Murder and A Merry Christmas

Cherryville Cozy Mysteries, Volume 1

Ellie McDougan

Published by Cherryville Titles, 2022.

MURDER AND A MERRY CHRISTMAS

First edition. December 5, 2022.

Copyright © 2022 Ellie McDougan.

ISBN: 978-0645667417

Written by Ellie McDougan.

Table of Contents

Chapter 1...1

Chapter 2...6

Chapter 3...11

Chapter 4...16

Chapter 5...22

Chapter 6...27

Chapter 7...32

Chapter 8...38

Chapter 9...44

Chapter 10 49

Chapter 11 55

Chapter 12 60

Chapter 13 66

Chapter 14 72

Chapter 15 77

Chapter 16 82

Chapter 17 88

Chapter 18 94

Chapter 19 100

Chapter 20 106

Chapter 21 | Homicide and a Happy New Year. | Coming soon!.. 112

I'd like to give a big thanks to my INF writing buddies for being there. Beth, Paola, Teal, Alix and Clare. I couldn't have done it without you! You made your weird lights shine bright so that other wierdos, like me, could find you.

Also, thank you to those who beta-read my typo-ridden drafts with enthusiasm and encouragement, including my INF writing buddies, Dr. Elizabeth Houlihan and my Beta-reader and Copyediter, Nichole Heydenburg.

Chapter 1

"And I want five marshmallows," said the little girl loudly, the bobble on her woolen hat wobbling as she became more enthused. "Mommy said I could have five marshmallows!"

Light snowflakes dusted the rustic serving planks of the hot chocolate booth and the girl's hat. Belle Beaumont tugged at her own, more flattering, red woolen hat and smiled down at the little girl.

"Um, I can't fit five marshmallows into the cup, sweetie," she said, trying her best to remain patient. She should have closed up now. But another forty minutes wouldn't hurt anything. "The cups only hold four. And you need some space for the hot chocolate."

"But I want five and if you only put four inside, then I won't be able to count them on all of my fingers," the girl said, stamping her miniature boots in the snow and preparing to howl.

Belle's smile faltered somewhat.

"Okay, okay," she said, thinking quickly. "I'll do one marshmallow on top of your hot chocolate and put the other four marshmallows in their own cup. Would that work for you?"

The girl's face lit up. "Thank you! And could I have extra cream too?" she asked, her eyes widening with hope.

Belle didn't have any cream. She braced herself for a kiddie tantrum as she reached into the camping fridge for a bottle of whole milk.

"How about we start with milk?" she asked brightly as she unscrewed the top.

The girl nodded eagerly, and Belle poured a healthy dollop of milk into her cup before adding a large spoon of the bubbling hot chocolate from the Crock-Pot to the milk and stirring.

"I'm Belle, by the way. What's your name?"

"My mommy told me not to speak to strangers," the girl said, her little face serious. "But I can speak to you because you're working in the hot chocolate booth." Belle's heart melted a little. "That's very sensible

1

of your mommy," she said, passing the girl her drink, hoping that she did not have to answer to this little girl's mommy. "Your cup's hot. Be careful."

The girl nodded, handed Belle a few coins, and sipped her hot chocolate. "It's so yummy," she squealed. Then she picked up the extra paper cup with four marshmallows and carried her treat into the small forest of Christmas trees up the hill, joining her parents as they chose the perfect tree to decorate.

Belle watched her go, wondering if she'd made a mistake in giving away four marshmallows to someone who clearly didn't need any extra sugar. Just before dinnertime, too. But that was for the little girl's mommy to figure out.

It was four-thirty and Belle had been working at the tree farm since seven-thirty that morning, running the hot chocolate booth for the stream of customers arriving to select a tree. Her feet ached.

And no wonder! Business had been booming at the tree farm for over a week. Almost half of the stock had already been sold, a lot of it wholesale to businesses who sent trucks to collect large orders. Hundreds of trees had also been carefully selected by excited families and taken back to cozy homes for decorating. Right now, a few families were still wandering about, looking at the remaining trees while Christmas carols played loudly over the outdoor speakers. The remaining harvested trees stood in regimented rows, their roots wrapped in neat plastic balls, ready for replanting after Christmas.

Belle sighed and rested her chin on a gloved hand.

The sound of crunching boots came from behind her. She turned with a smile toward the customer. Except it wasn't a customer. It was her boss and the owner of the tree farm.

"Hey, Harvey," she said, straightening up and pulling her woolen hat lower over her forehead and ponytail to keep warm. "What are you still doing here?"

Harvey was a small, balding man in his fifties with an enthusiasm for Christmas that belied his stature. He wore red suspenders on his khakis.

"Just making sure everything's okay," he said. "The booth has been doing good business today, I hope?"

She nodded and wiped down the serving counter with a cloth. "Yeah, but you don't need to check on me. I'll be done by six."

"I know. I wanted to say hello. And that you're doing a good job. The booth has been very popular."

Last year, the local women's guild ran the booth. However, there had been so many arguments about the hot chocolate recipe that the entire operation had been a disaster. Even now, some of the older women at the Cherryville Women's Guild still refused to speak to each other.

"I'm glad it worked out," she said. "Thank you again for the job."

"Okay, well... just sorting out the accounting for the night." He handed her an envelope. "Here's your pay for today."

Belle looked inside and saw several dollars more than she expected. "Harvey, I can't keep this," she said, aghast.

He waved his hands and shook his head fiercely. "If you leave it with me, I'll put it in the Christmas fund jar. You've been a lifesaver this year. I don't know what we would have done without you. Your hot chocolate has made the place feel more like Christmas. Last year, the ladies from the women's guild scared off half of my customers..." He pulled a comical face.

She looked at the envelope in her hands and smiled, shoving it inside her jacket pocket. The monthly mortgage payment for her grandmother's house was due soon. Then, of course, there were her grandmother's medical bills. After the last round of treatment, the cancer was now undetectable. However, all the medical bills still needed to be paid according to a payment plan arrangement that Belle had signed with the hospital.

"Thank you," she said. "You've done so much for me since I moved back here."

It was true. Belle was twenty-eight years old and had expected to be pursuing her career in the city. But she had only worked at an office job in the city for the last two years before she had received a call from the hospital. Gram hadn't told her about the cancer diagnosis because she didn't want to worry her granddaughter. It was so typical of her grandmother. As soon as she had heard the news, Belle had moved back home immediately, back to Cherryville.

"Well, you're welcome. And if anyone asks for the best hot chocolate around, you tell them that they can only get it at Harvey's Tree Farm."

She laughed and shook her head. A warm feeling swelled in her chest. She could not remember any previous boss telling her to be proud of something that she'd done.

"Are you going along to the Christmas Carol Singalong?" she asked. The Singalong was scheduled to be held in the old town market square the next week.

"Absolutely. I am the one supplying the town Christmas tree, remember?" he chuckled. "I better make sure that it looks good on the night or there will be hell to pay. Since I refused them the running of the hot chocolate booth this year, I can't mess up the Singalong. Can you imagine? The Women's Guild will blackball me for good."

"Harvey," a voice called from down the path towards the parking lot. "Harvey, we need you to sign for the new shipment of lights."

Harvey looked over his shoulder at the lot and then back to Belle. "Sorry, but I need to go do that now," he said, adjusting his red suspenders. "Can I ask you for another cup of that hot chocolate to go?"

Belle grinned at him. "Sure, no problem," she said. "Here, take this," she said brightly, handing him a hot chocolate topped with one of the larger marshmallows.

"Thanks, Belle," he said. "And you have a very Merry Christmas."

She watched as he walked away and couldn't help but smile at his excitement about Christmas. Harvey had been working for years to make something of his small tree farm and it seemed like this year was finally going to be a success. And her booth had helped! At first, Belle had been worried that his idea of selling hot chocolate would fall flat like it had the previous year, but for once everything seemed to be going right. Not only was her hot chocolate attracting customers for his farm but Harvey was paying her a wage and letting her keep the profit that she made from all the hot chocolate that she sold. She watched Harvey out of the corner of her eye as he helped a customer carry a shipment of lights. She knew that he regularly helped out at the local soup kitchen and had also hired several men who had served prison time, when nobody else would, just to help them get back on their feet. The man was the quintessential kindly uncle of the entire town.

The lump of the envelope now stuffed in her jacket pocket caused a bubble of guilt to rise in her chest. Harvey should be keeping his money to pay for his farm. Then she thought about her grandmother's medical bills and her mortgage and sighed. She didn't have any other option than to accept Harvey's generosity.

Stirring the chocolate slowly, Belle hummed along to the cheerful Christmas music as she watched the throng of customers choosing their Christmas trees.

Chapter 2

The next day dawned bright and clear. It was one of those sunny winter mornings where the sky was a cloudless blue and there was little humidity in the air. The cold air smelled minty fresh, and the wind had stilled. Everything was covered in powdered snow, the houses, the cars, and the trees; it all sat under a thick coating of pristine white.

Belle continued to hum the same Christmas Carol as she walked to her car. The music from the day before was now perpetually stuck in her head. She fumbled with her keys for a moment before finding the right one and unlocking the door. Getting in, she started up the engine and let it warm up and sputter in the cold morning air while she applied some lip-gloss.

It was Saturday, just over a week before Christmas, and Belle expected it to be one of the busiest days at the Christmas Tree Farm yet. If it were anywhere else, she would have expected that anyone that was going to buy a tree would have done it already. But these were Harvey's trees and people would still be arriving at the farm right up until Christmas Day. Harvey's trees were well known for being top quality. Harvey grew his trees in a special way and then, instead of cutting them down, sold them with a root ball, ready for planting in the garden or in a pot once the holidays were over. Plus, from what Belle had heard, it sounded like Christmas trees were in short supply this year. People were coming from far and wide just to grab what they could find.

The drive to Harvey's Christmas Tree Farm was short, and Belle was soon pulling into a parking spot in the car lot. Her shift only officially started at eight o'clock but she always arrived at seven sharp. She got out and locked the door, then made her way over to the entrance. The path from the car park had already been shoveled and Belle's boots crunched on the leftover sprinkling of snow as she walked to the hot chocolate booth. Harvey had purposely positioned the booth near the entrance, to lure customers directly in with a warm drink.

She was already dusting snow off the hot chocolate booth with a broomstick when Harvey drove up.

He blew the horn of his truck and waved cheerfully as he got out to open his office and set up for another day's trading. "Good morning, Belle!" Harvey called. "Looking forward to a busy day today?"

Belle grinned and set down her broom, leaning it against the counter. "Sure am. I have even more decorations for the booth. I thought that it needed something extra. Plus, I wanted to get the Crock-Pot set up with a batch of chocolate before the rush starts."

Harvey nodded. "Good idea. It is going to be crazy again today, mind yourself!" He picked up his toolbox and walked over to the little office trailer. "I will bring some more lights for you to hang up if you want," he called over his shoulder as he went into his office.

While Belle waited for Harvey to return with the promised lights, she fetched a couple of boxes of decorations from her station wagon. She had seen them at the second-hand store in town and had thought that they would be perfect for her booth. Setting the boxes down in the snow, she proceeded to unpack them like treasures. There were thick ropes of tinsel; a variety of red and gold bows; a box full of glittery plastic snowflakes; and a garland to string across the booth's doorway for decoration. Belle arranged them all, stepping back now and then to admire her handiwork.

She was just in the process of hanging another strand of tinsel when Harvey returned with a bundle of lights. "Here you go," he said, handing them over. "Love the tinsel!" Then he trotted off to check on the music and figure out why the Christmas Carols were not yet playing.

"Thank you!" Belle called after him. She set the lights up in a pleasing fashion and stepped back to admire them once more. They twinkled amidst the tinsel and against the rustic wood of the booth.

Belle decided to hang a few plastic snowflakes around the lights. Harvey walked past just as she was sticking up the last one. "Perfect!" he said, nodding his head in approval of her work, just as the sound system came on and started playing upbeat Christmas music.

While Belle had been setting up the decorations, the Crock-Pot had begun bubbling with rich chocolate goodness. She turned the heat down and added some cinnamon and an extra cup of cocoa powder.

Before long, various vehicles started arriving. Customers had driven from all over the country to get their trees. The parking lot was getting busier and busier by the minute as more and more people looked for parking spaces.

The morning rush had begun.

For several hours, Belle worked hard, serving piping hot mugs of delicious chocolate to all comers. Harvey had been right, it certainly was a busy day. The rich aroma of sweet cocoa wafted around the immediate area of the booth and, together with the sound of the Christmas carols over the speakers, added an inviting ambiance to the entrance of the farm.

The morning went by in a blur, as Belle served one customer after another. She needed to refill the Crock-Pot several times and, by her calculations, she had already served over a hundred customers by lunchtime. Taking a few minutes to unwrap the packed lunch that her grandmother had prepared for her, she wolfed down her sandwich.

Meanwhile, Harvey and the men who helped him were hauling huge trees up onto customers' trailers and roof racks and helping to tie them down, ready for the trip back to waiting houses. They would be decorated with all sorts of Christmas decorations ranging from homemade baubles to store-bought tinsel. Belle imagined all the little kids helping their folks decorate this year's trees and her heart flushed with warmth.

By the end of the day, Belle's feet ached again but she still had an hour to go before she could close up for the night. She had long since lost count of the numbers of mugs of hot chocolate that she had served.

Finally, there were no more customers waiting for hot chocolate and she took advantage of one of the rare moments of quiet to quickly visit the lady's bathroom again. Catching sight of herself in the mirror, she gasped. Her face was flushed, and her long chestnut hair had gone a little frizzy, sticking up in different directions. She took a few moments to fix her hair, then crammed her woolen hat back on.

As Belle exited the lady's bathroom, she clapped her gloved hands together and hugged herself as the temperature dropped. A shiver ran down her spine as a gust of cold air whipped around her. The chill in the air felt sharp on her skin. She tried to shield her head from the cold but her hat did little to keep her warm. Still, it was better than nothing.

The walk back to the booth was short but something made her pause. Snippets of angry voices flitted by in the breeze. Belle's eyes darted toward the office. The voices sounded out of place in the Christmas ambiance and it was difficult to tell where they came from.

Belle glanced around. Other than a single expensive SUV and some trucks, the parking lot was more or less empty. A couple of late customers were looking at the Christmas lights section.

Her breath plumed out in front of her. She waited for a moment, listening to the voices again. One was definitely Harvey—she could hear the deep thrum of his voice, even from where she stood. And another voice that was softer and more higher-pitched. A woman's voice.

Perhaps someone was unhappy with a Christmas tree that they bought?

Or worse, perhaps they were unhappy with their hot chocolate!

She had served so many happy customers throughout the day. What if someone had not liked their hot chocolate? Belle anxiously cast her mind back to the customers she had served. She hadn't heard this any customers complaining.

After some indecision, she gritted her teeth decisively, walked the short distance from the car lot to the pre-fabricated office, and peeped around the corner.

Two figures were silhouetted against the light spilling from the open office door. Harvey and a woman. The woman wore a large mulberry colored coat tied around her waist and her black hair billowed out around her face. Belle could not tell who it was, but their conversation sounded like a heated debate.

The wind blew again, and Belle held her breath as words carried on the air. "But you agreed," Harvey said. He turned slightly and for a moment, Belle caught sight of his face. He looked angrier than she had ever seen him before.

"These things happen," said the woman, her tone sharp. "I don't know why you're making such a big deal out of it."

"Well, I am and you shouldn't be here at all," replied Harvey.

Belle stepped back. Whatever was going on, it looked private, and she didn't want to intrude. She turned around and then walked briskly back to her booth.

Hopefully, whatever the argument was about, it was just a private thing and not about the business. Whatever it was, she that hoped that it would not affect her job at the tree farm. She really needed this work to last until Christmas.

Chapter 3

Belle returned to her booth with her mind in a whirl. Who on earth had Harvey been arguing with outside of his office?

The Crock-Pot was now empty and cold and there were no customers around. The temperature was dropping. The sky became darker as snowflakes swirled around her. Belle quickly packed up for the day, even though it was twenty minutes sooner than she had planned to.

She wiped down all of the surfaces in the booth, packing the Christmas decorations carefully in the boxes. It was a bit of a hike back and forth to her unlocked car to stow all of her stuff away. It would be easier to leave the decorations up overnight but she knew that they would all be covered with snow in the morning. Shoveling snow off the booth was more work than just packing it up every night. Plus, Belle liked everything to look fresh every morning.

As she worked, Belle wondered who the mystery woman was. There were many people in Cherryville that she didn't know. However, she had seen most of the town residents, sufficient to recognize them from a distance at least. Belle could not think of anyone in Cherryville who had long black hair and who wore an elegant coat. In fact, she couldn't think of anyone who lived in town who could afford a coat like that at all.

And what had they been arguing about?

It had sounded like the woman had broken an agreement. But that was all that Belle had managed to piece together from the few words that she had overheard. She shook her head.

What does it matter? It's none of my business who Harvey does business with.

Belle's stomach grumbled loudly, her sandwich from lunch long gone. It was dinner time and her grandmother's cooking would be waiting for her. The thought of it made her stomach grumble even more.

She resolutely put the mystery woman out of her mind while she locked up for the night. As she was taking the last of the decorations down from the booth, Belle noticed that a strand of tinsel had gone missing. It was the new thick red strand of tinsel that she had wrapped around the small pole on the counter.

"Silly thing must have blown off in the wind." She looked around the entrance of the farm. But it wasn't there.

Or maybe someone took it?

The thought annoyed Belle more than it should have. She'd enjoyed that strand of tinsel—it matched the red ribbon that she used to tie up her hair for work this morning. After hearing those angry voices, the missing strand put a small damper on her mood.

"Some people are just rude," she grumbled.

Pulling the tarp over the booth, she fastened it onto the ready-made hooks. Then she gathered up the empty packets that she had emptied of cocoa powder. Tomorrow, she would need to bring more from her supplies at home.

As she trudged her way to her trusty station wagon, she clapped her gloved hands together and hugged herself. Her breath made small clouds of mist as she breathed out. Shivering slightly, Belle opened the unlocked back door of her car and placed the last box on one side before getting into the driver's seat and closing the door.

She reached into her pocket for her car keys but came up empty. "Oh great, just what I need." Catching sight of her reflection in the rearview mirror, she rolled her eyes.

Belle rummaged through the various items in the passenger seat and the glove compartment. But the car keys weren't there! Groaning, she remembered where she had last seen them—at the side of the sink in the lady's bathroom as she washed her hands and fixed her hair.

She thought wistfully of the fireplace at her grandmother's house which would be flickering with a cozy fire. A warm dinner would be waiting in the oven. Gram had promised her a special dinner tonight as a celebration for doing so well at the chocolate booth. And there was nothing as delicious as her grandmother's bourbon stew. Except, possibly her grandmother's roast chicken dinners.

Sighing loudly, Belle climbed back out of the station wagon. She walked as quickly as she could through the snow back to the lady's bathroom.

In the distance, a group of men who had helped Harvey with the trees during the day stood around a campfire. They laughed and drank something warm from their dented camping mugs.

The campfire fizzed and crackled as someone tossed pine cones onto it and the homely scent of a burning log fire drifted about. Many of the men had driven big trucks to the farm that morning and then had spent the day harvesting trees and loading up. They would head back out first thing in the morning. The rest were locals who helped Harvey with the heavy lifting. Harvey often hired men that desperately needed the work, including ex-convicts who were trying to get back on their feet.

Belle reached the bathroom, placed her hand on the cold metal door handle, and turned it. Stepping out of the wind, she shut the door behind her.

"There they are!" she said, spotting her car keys right where she had left them. She stretched out a gloved hand and quickly scooped them up, dropping them in her jacket pocket.

Exiting the bathroom, Belle headed back to the station wagon again. She was determined not to let such a little thing as forgetting her keys stand between her and her grandmother's bourbon stew.

But her brain kept turning over the memory of the angry words that Harvey had exchanged with the mystery woman.

It had sounded like they knew each other. However, Belle couldn't think of anyone who would argue with Harvey. Of course, there would always be customers ready to complain. But an argument like that was out of the ordinary.

So, who was she?

Belle frowned, feeling quite protective of Cherryville's friendly, middle-aged tree farmer. He had given her a job when she needed it and she wanted to do right by him. If he was arguing with someone, then surely it would be for a good reason?

The wind picked up and pulled at a piece of plastic covering some of the Christmas trees. It fluttered in the swirling air currents for a moment before being pulled free and floating across the pathway. Belle couldn't let it blow away into the nearby forest and immediately jogged after it. Grabbing the plastic, Belle scrunched it into a ball, and looked around for a dumpster.

There were two nearby. Large bins that were almost as tall as she was. The metal lid of the first was firmly closed. She had no choice but to use the other one. She heaved open the heavy lid and prepared to toss the balled-up plastic sheet into the dumpster.

Then Belle froze.

A flash of red caught her eye. There, tangled amidst Christmas tree trimmings, was a thick rope of red tinsel.

So, this is where it went!

Belle reached out and tugged at it, grateful to have found her missing tinsel again.

Then she frowned. Underneath the tinsel and tree trimmings was a familiar color: a mulberry color. And it looked very much like the color of the coat that Belle had seen a stranger wearing an hour earlier. She reached out a gloved hand again but before she could touch the fabric in the dumpster, the wind caught the end of the red tinsel and swirled it away, revealing the shape of an arm.

She squeaked and jumped backward.

"Oh, my goodness!"

It was the arm of a woman. In the dumpster. Or at least, that it looked like the arm of a woman. She could not see much more than the mulberry fabric and the red tinsel tangled with bits of discarded Christmas trees. Nonetheless, it looked like part of a woman who wasn't moving.

In fact, it looked like the woman that Belle had seen arguing with Harvey.

Chapter 4

Is she sleeping? Or has she passed out?

Belle stared at the dumpster.

When she saw no movement at all, a terrible thought formed in her mind. She gasped and covered her mouth with a gloved hand, then stared at the coat for a long moment to see if the woman stirred.

She didn't.

Belle's mind raced. Looking around quickly, Belle saw light spilling from the windows of Harvey's office. She spun on her heel and hurried to the office door.

Knocking loudly, she called out Harvey's name.

"Come in," he called back.

With an effort, Belle forced the heavy door open against the wind and stepped inside to find Harvey sitting behind his desk. He looked up at her with a smile on his face.

"Belle," he said warmly. "What can I do for you?" Then, as he caught sight of her shocked face, he frowned. "What's wrong?"

"Harvey," Belle stammered. "You...you have to come and look. I think there's a woman in your dumpster."

He laughed. "Who climbs in a dumpster in this weather? Did she drop something?"

"No, Harvey, I think that she's dead."

Harvey's face drained of all color. "What?"

"Come with me," Belle urged, turning back toward the door. "I can't explain it. What are we going to do?" She was trying not to panic, but she had never seen a dead body before.

Harvey followed Belle outside and together they hurried the short distance to the dumpster area, through the falling snow.

As they drew closer to the dumpster, Belle could see the mulberry-colored material again. It was definitely clothing, now dusted with snowflakes.

Harvey walked up to the dumpster and peered inside. Then he gasped. "Geez." Harvey cleared some of the pine branches covering the top half of the woman's prone form and frowned. "I think you're right."

"Do you know who it is?" Belle asked, her face as pale as the falling snow. She looked at the woman's lifeless body with a shudder. The stranger's face was hidden, and Belle could only see the back of her head.

Harvey stood gazing into the dumpster as if in more shock than Belle had been.

"Harvey? Are you okay?"

"We need to call the police," he replied curtly, wiping his eyes and sniffing. "I'll check around for anything suspicious. You better call the sheriff." He looked around, taking in their surroundings. "Be careful."

Nodding nervously, Belle pulled her phone out of her pocket. The battery was low, and the reception wasn't great. A shiver ran down Belle's spine as she remembered the swirl of red tinsel caught by the wind that had first caught her attention. It probably was the missing strand of red tinsel from her booth, but she couldn't be sure. After all, one piece of tinsel looked very much like another, and Harvey sold tinsel at the farm.

"Call them now. I'm going to check out who else is still here and tell them what's going on," Harvey said hurriedly, stepping away from the dumpster. He turned and quickly jogged over to the men standing around the campfire.

Belle watched him talking to the men for a moment before she noticed the goosebumps rising all over her arms and shoulders. She rubbed at her arms, feeling the chill of the surrounding air, then pulled off her glove so she could use her mobile phone.

Tapping in the number for the local police station, Belle waited impatiently. Finally, after a few moments of ringing, someone answered. "Cherryville Police Station," said a gruff voice. Belle recognized the sheriff's voice straight away.

"Sheriff, it's Belle."

"Belle? Nice to hear from you. Is everything okay?"

"No. I'm calling on behalf of Harvey. There's a woman in the dumpster behind his office. She isn't moving. I think she may be dead." Her voice faltered. She looked over at the scene around the campfire, but could see no sign of Harvey or any of the other men he had been talking to. They must have spread out the check the area. "You need to come here right away. I'm behind Harvey's office at his tree farm."

"Okay," the sheriff drawled. "I'll be right there. Stay where you are and make sure no one touches anything."

There was a click, and Belle listened to a dial tone. She closed her phone, wondering if it was too cold to go back inside Harvey's office until the police arrived. All she wanted to do was go home, curl up under her blanket, and hide. Her appetite seemed to have deserted her.

While she waited, she paced up and down, looking on the ground for anything that would shed some light on what had happened. But there was nothing to see other than the mulberry coat and the trailing rope of red tinsel that had uncoiled itself and was now blowing in the wind. The falling snow had long since covered her own footprints, and anyone else's.

Well, at least Harvey will know something. After all, he was speaking with the poor woman an hour ago. I'll let him speak to the police.

Belle stamped her feet to keep warm. She pulled her coat tighter around her, wishing that she had worn an extra layer of clothing. She suddenly thought of her grandmother waiting for her and wondering why she was late for dinner. Lifting her phone, she quickly called home. "Hello, Gram?" Belle asked. "It's me."

"Belle! Where are you? You said you would be home ages ago!" Belle could hear the worry in Grace Beaumont's voice.

"I know. I'm sorry. But there's been a bit of an incident here at work," Belle said in a rush. "We had to call the sheriff and I have to wait until he gets here. I found a woman in the dumpster. We think... well, we think that she is no longer alive."

"No longer alive?" The shock in her grandmother's voice was palpable. "Do you mean that you have found a *dead body*? Good heavens! Are you okay? Are you safe?"

"I'm fine, Gram. But I have to stay and wait for the sheriff to come. He wants to talk with me because I'm the one that found her."

Her grandmother huffed. "What happened? Was there an accident? Harvey is usually so careful with his workers. Who is she?"

"I don't know, Gram. I have no idea. Harvey asked me to call the sheriff, and that's what I did. He's already gone to talk to his crew. I think they are checking the area for anyone who shouldn't be here." Belle pulled her jacket collar up, feeling the icy wind on her neck. "I'm supposed to stay nearby."

"Okay, well, dinner is ready, and if the sheriff doesn't get there soon, I'll come over there myself to make sure that you don't catch a cold in this weather."

Belle could hear Mittens meowing in the background, the sound that he made when he could smell Gram's cooking and was hoping for the scraps. Mittens was a stray that had showed up at the door a few years ago and had decided to stay.

"Thank you, Gram. But I'll be fine," Belle said in a rush. "I'll call you when the sheriff is done talking to me."

"Okay," her grandmother answered, concerned. "You be safe and try to stay warm in this awful wind."

"I will," Belle promised. She ended the call and tucked her phone in her pocket.

Footsteps crunched in the snow behind her, and Belle jumped, whirling around to see who was there. But it was just Harvey and two guys from the campfire. Belle vaguely remembered meeting them on her first day. One was tall and skinny and the other one was short and bald with a round, friendly face.

"Are you okay? We checked the perimeter but couldn't find anything," said Jerry, the short guy, with a worried expression. "Harvey said that..." He gasped as he looked behind Belle. "...you found a body." He walked up to the dumpster and stared inside.

"Yes, the police should be here in a minute," Belle said. The cold air was making her teeth chatter.

As if on cue, the flash of lights on the sheriff's car came down the road outside the farm. The car turned into the parking lot of the Christmas tree farm and crunched on the snow until it pulled up nearby. The sheriff got out, followed by another police officer.

Sheriff Barnes was a tall, imposing man and Belle sighed in relief at the sight of him. He was someone everyone in town turned to. He would know what to do. She gave him a small wave, and he nodded at her, then waved the other officer over.

"Belle," said the sheriff as he approached. "Show me what you found."

"Over there," she replied, pointing. "I didn't touch anything, only the lid of the dumpster that I propped up against the wall. And Harvey moved some of those branches." She pointed to the discarded tree trimmings.

The sheriff's brow furrowed as he took in the scene. "You touched nothing else?"

"No," Belle replied nervously. "I ran to Harvey to get help."

The sheriff walked over to the dumpster and looked inside. He said something to his deputy, then came back.

"Any idea how long the body has been there?" he asked Belle.

She shook her head. "No. I only noticed her when I came out here to go to the lady's bathroom and then to throw away this piece of plastic..." Belle's voice trailed off and she realized she was still holding the plastic under her arm that she had meant to throw away when she had opened the dumpster and saw the mulberry fabric.

"Did you notice any footprints leading to or away from the dumpster?" asked the sheriff, taking the plastic and looking at it closely.

Belle shook her head again. "No, it was already snowing when I arrived, so whatever footprints were there are gone by now."

"Do you know who this woman is?"

Belle shook her head again. "No. She is definitely not from around here. But I'm sure Harvey will be able to tell you more about her than me." She gestured to her boss, who now stood nearby.

Sheriff Barnes nodded. "Okay. Give your details to Officer Derek. Then you can go home. Thanks, Belle."

Chapter 5

Even though she knew that he would already know who she was, Belle gave Officer Derek her details, including her full name and phone number, and told him that she was running the hot chocolate booth at Harvey's Christmas Tree Farm over the holidays. She went through the events of the last few hours while Derek obligingly wrote it all down in a little notebook. He was a pleasant fellow and concerned about her welfare. She remembered him from junior high.

"I'm sorry that I can't be of more help," she said. "But, like I said, if I remember anything else, I'll let you know."

"Thanks." He nodded and moved aside so she could walk to her car.

Belle walked past the sheriff, who was asking Harvey questions. Poor Harvey looked ashen.

As Belle passed, she overheard the sheriff speaking. "And so, you've never seen this woman before?" he asked, pointing at the dumpster.

"Never," Harvey confirmed. "I've never seen her before in my life."

Belle almost stumbled in the snow.

Never in his life? But he was just speaking to her a couple of hours ago!

"Are you sure?" Sheriff Barnes asked.

Harvey nodded and looked like he was sweating, even though the temperature was dropping. "I'm sure." His eyes darted back and forth between the sheriff and the dumpster. He coughed and then appeared to blow his nose on a tissue, almost as if he was crying.

Wow! What's going on here?

Belle widened her eyes as she quickly climbed into her car. She pulled the door closed as she started the engine. Switching the heat on, she rubbed her hands together while she waited for the car to warm up.

Focusing on getting home, she turned on the radio and the sounds of Christmas carols filled the car as the heat warmed her cold feet. Then she confirmed her phone was still in her pocket in case Officer Derek or Sheriff Barnes needed to call her. She put the car into gear and drove out of the parking lot.

She made her way slowly back to town, windshield wipers swishing away the snowflakes. The drive to her grandmother's house took a little longer than expected with the falling snow and she drove carefully, her lights on bright.

As she passed the houses and storefronts in town, she marveled at the Christmas decorations up on the buildings and visible in the windows. There were lights, snowmen, and Santa Claus figurines propped up outside. The windows were lit on the inside with cozy candles and many people had set their Christmas trees close to the glass so that the little Christmas tree lights could blink against the frosted panes.

The town streets looked lovely with twinkling lights in the bare trees. Belle felt a pang when she thought about how a few hours ago an unknown woman had ended up dead. Discarded in a dumpster, alone but for a swirl of tinsel.

She shivered. She was cold, even with the car heater blowing air on full blast. If only she could get warm, then she could think more clearly and figure out what had happened.

What a day! First, she had sold a record amount of hot chocolate. Then she had discovered a dead body. And then Harvey had lied to the police. At the Christmas Tree Farm, of all places.

Harvey was an upstanding town resident, and he had a reputation for running a wholesome, friendly business. Everyone knew him to be an honest fellow that helped anyone in need. Belle was certainly grateful that he had given her the job of running the hot chocolate booth.

"I can't believe that he would lie," Belle whispered. "He wouldn't. But then he definitely knows that woman."

Harvey may not be telling the police the whole truth, but Belle also knew that she couldn't tell the police that either. She couldn't betray

Harvey. And, what would she say anyway? That she had somehow been hanging around his office listening to his private conversation?

Belle parked her station wagon outside her grandmother's house, locked up, and headed inside. She was relieved to find her grandmother in the kitchen, making a cup of tea.

Mittens rushed over and rubbed himself against her legs. "Hello, Mittens." She patted him on the head and he trotted off again, happy for some attention from one of his favorite humans.

His life as a stray long forgotten, Mittens had adapted well to a life in a warm house with a constant supply of food.

"There you are, dear," said Grace Beaumont with a worried frown as she came over to give her a hug. "Are you okay?"

"Hi Gram," Belle said as she removed her coat and boots. "Sorry I'm late."

"It's all right," she said while looking at Belle over her glasses. "Now, tell me again what happened. You look tired."

Belle smiled wearily and nodded.

"Yes," she said with a sigh. Then she sat down at the table and wrapped her icy hands around the waiting cup of steaming tea.

Her grandmother pulled up another chair and sat down.

"I have been talking to the neighbors, and they said they heard from their cousin that someone was murdered at the farm," her grandmother said. She took off her glasses and rubbed them with the hem of her cardigan.

Belle looked at her grandmother in disbelief. "Already?" she asked, shocked.

"Oh yes," Grace said with a nod of her head. "Gossip travels fast in this town. That's why I prefer to get it straight from the horse's mouth."

"Well, I only know a little," Belle said. "The police are there right now; they're questioning Harvey."

"That is understandable," Grace said. She still looked shaken by this news. "But how will he know anything about it?"

Belle pursed her lips. "Actually, he may know more than anyone," she said again. She quickly filled her grandmother in on everything that had happened that evening. She told her about overhearing Harvey and about the woman arguing. And about how Harvey had told the police he had never seen the woman before. "I think I figure out what happened first before going to the police with what I saw. What do you think?"

"This all sounds very strange," Grace commented in a low voice. "Perhaps you should not be getting involved, Belle."

Belle looked at her grandmother and groaned. "I can't stand by and not do anything," she said. "Harvey is a family friend and completely harmless. He has helped us so much. I can't believe he would hurt anyone. And he looked so worried."

Grace smiled as she picked up the teapot, refilled Belle's cup, and then topped off her own before returning it to the table.

"Well, I hope that you handle it carefully," Grace said as she stirred a teaspoon of sugar into her tea. "Your curiosity sometimes gets the better of you and I wouldn't want to see you hurt."

Belle smiled gratefully at her grandmother. "I'll be careful," she said before taking a sip of her tea.

She watched as Grace bustled about the kitchen, opening the oven and taking out two bowls of food that had been keeping warm. They were filled with large servings of her famous savory stew, thick with vegetables.

Belle exclaimed that it was too much to eat, while her mouth watered at the sight of it.

"Nonsense," said Grace as she placed the bowls on the table. "You must keep up your strength, girl. Besides, this is a celebration because you've been doing so well at that hot chocolate booth. Even though some strange things have happened today, we still need to celebrate the small things."

Belle grinned as her grandmother sat down and joined her at the table.

Belle nodded in agreement before picking up her spoon.

The events of the evening receded as Belle tucked into the dinner she had been looking forward to all day. She savored each mouthful of food. She looked across the table at her grandmother, who was eating with gusto, making Belle smile.

Afterward, Belle insisted on clearing up while her grandmother dosed in front of the fire. She dried the dishes and utensils, setting them neatly in their places, before wiping down the countertop.

As she cleaned up, Belle's mind flickered back over what had happened earlier. She thought about the woman in the dumpster, wondering who she was and why she had been arguing with Harvey. Why had her boss not mentioned it to the police? He must have had a good reason. Which could only mean one thing: her friendly boss may be in trouble.

Despite telling herself that it was better left alone, Belle had already decided that there was only one thing to do. Before she spoke to Sheriff Barnes about what she saw that evening, she would investigate further and find out what had happened for herself. She owed Harvey that much, at least.

Chapter 6

Belle awoke to the smell of gingerbread and cinnamon. She stretched lazily and yawned.

Last night had been colder than usual. However, it had taken longer than normal to get to sleep. After tossing and turning for what felt like hours, she had finally fallen into a deep sleep under the heavy patchwork quilt that her grandmother had made when she had first joined the Women's Guild.

Belle's dreams, however, had been full of images of the dead woman and her mulberry coat, while a strand of red tinsel blew in the wind. She awoke feeling foggy-headed. It was as if her brain kept trying to figure out what she should do next, even in her dreams. So far, it hadn't come up with anything useful.

What am I going to do?

Her brain kept turning the problem over in her mind. But she still had no idea why Harvey wasn't telling the police about his argument with the mystery women or how to go about investigating who she was.

Mittens, noticing that Belle had finally sat up, jumped onto her bed and pushed his head under her hand.

"Good morning, you little ball of fluff," she said, momentarily distracted from her thoughts. "Goodness! Is that the time? I can't believe that you let me sleep so late! Have you already had your breakfast?"

Mittens licked his lips and purred.

"Okay, I'll take that as a yes." Belle swung her legs out of bed and got up, grabbing her robe from the back of the chair. "I'll make some tea and see what Gram is up to."

Belle pulled on her fluffy slippers and dressing gown and wandered downstairs to the kitchen. "Good morning, Gram. That smells amazing."

Grace Beaumont bustled about her kitchen in her slippers, her grey hair in curlers. She opened the oven, letting out a blast of warm air and a cloud of fragrant steam. Belle had to admit that her grandmother made the best gingerbread in town.

"Oh, good morning, Belle! How did you sleep?"

"Not bad, all things considered." Belle set the kettle on the stove and waited for it to boil. She set up her favorite mug and selected a berry tea bag from the tin her grandmother kept on the windowsill. She took a seat at the kitchen table while she waited for the kettle to sing. "I'm worried about Harvey, though. How do we figure out who that poor woman was? And why isn't he telling the police everything he knows?"

Gram raised an eyebrow. "We? We don't need to figure anything out. Sheriff Barnes is on the case. I'm sure everything will work out fine. You'll see." She pointed at the kitchen table. "Now, I baked a ton of gingerbread this morning for the raffle. It is going to be the best one yet."

Every year, Cherryville hosted a Christmas Carol Singalong, and every year it got better and better. Whoever was in charge of organizing the Singalong tried to outdo the organizers from the previous year. This year was no different.

Last year, the bowling club had been in charge of organizing it. They had printed lovely little flyers and delivered them all over town. Some of their flyers had made it to the next town, Hollydale, inviting the residents in the surrounding areas to the Cherryville Christmas celebrations. The bowling club had even organized for the kids at the school to put on a play.

However, this year Hollydale had stepped up their game and sent their own flyers around, inviting Cherryville residents to a competing Singalong in Hollydale scheduled for the same evening. They were planning fireworks.

Those Hollydale flyers had caused quite a stir in the Women's Guild. In fact, it had caused such a stir that they had called a special meeting about it. It was decided that they needed to do something big to make sure Cherryville's Singalong wasn't only better than the year before, but better than anything Hollydale could possibly organize.

"Doris is coming over to help me make houses from all of this gingerbread. Would you like to join us?"

Doris was Grace's friend from the Women's Guild and the town seamstress. She was also the lackey of the President of the Women's Guild, Wilma Figg. Whenever there was something that needed to be done for an event in town, Wilma usually volunteered Doris to do it.

Then Doris asked Grace for help.

And this is how I end up getting sucked into these things.

Belle pulled her long chestnut hair into a messy bun and secured it with a hairband from her dressing gown pocket. "I can't leave the hot chocolate booth early today. Harvey has some big orders of decorations coming in today and so there will be a lot of customers coming for tree lights and stuff like that. Hopefully, they'll be customers who need mugs of hot chocolate to keep them warm."

"Oh well, what about after your shift ends? Doris and I will still be working on the gingerbread houses then."

The kettle whistled, and Belle got up to make her tea. She poured hot water into her mug and steeped her berry tea bag. "Sure, that sounds good. I can help then." She glanced at the many packets of sweets and chocolates on the counter and whistled. "Do you think you have enough sweets?" she said, drily. Her grandmother was clearly planning on sticking the entire inventory from a sweet shop onto the gingerbread when she built miniature houses out of it.

"Wonderful!" replied Grace, ignoring Belle's comment. "Oh, that reminds me! I thought you could offer to set up your hot chocolate booth at the Singalong this year."

Belle yawned again and shook her head. "Not so sure *that* would be a great idea. Wilma hasn't forgiven me for taking over the hot chocolate booth at Harvey's place. And you know how Harvey said the Women's Guild scared away half of his customers last year? Well, I sure hope that Wilma doesn't hear that he said that or we'll all be in heaps of trouble."

Wilma, the proud President of the Cherryville Women's Guild, was the most opinionated and irritating woman in town. She was always taking charge of organizing events in town and trying to make them more spectacular than they needed to be, usually with unintended and disastrous results.

Her grandmother nodded sympathetically. "Yes, I know Wilma can be annoying, but she's really just trying to help. The other ladies are quite fond of her."

Belle sighed and took a sip of her tea. "I know, Gram. It's just that she always seems to overplay things and then her plans fall apart."

Her grandmother patted her hand. "Don't worry, dear. I'm sure you'll be able to handle her. Just offer to set up your hot chocolate booth at the Singalong and she can't refuse you. A percentage of all of the profits goes to charity, after all. It would be hard for her to say no to that."

Belle took another sip of tea. "You're probably right. I'll think about it some more."

She stood up. "I'm going to get ready for work now. I'll be a bit late setting up as it is."

Her grandmother smiled. "Good girl. I will make you some of your favorite strawberry jam and toast for breakfast to go. And a packed lunch."

"Thanks." Belle kissed her on the cheek and headed back upstairs.

As Belle showered and dressed, she thought some more about what had happened the day before at Harvey's Christmas Farm.

How on earth am I going to find out who the mysterious woman is?

Surely, someone must have seen her before? Cherryville was rife with gossip. If anyone knew who the poor woman in the dumpster was, as sure as the sun rises, they would tell as many people in town as possible.

The trouble was that they would probably talk about Harvey too. In Belle's experience, small town gossip could take on a life of its own. The last thing that she wanted was for her boss to get caught up in it. She would have to be discreet in her questioning and try not to draw too much attention to herself or Harvey.

Belle sighed and finished getting ready for work. The fragrant scent of gingerbread reminded her of her grandmother's request that she set up the hot chocolate booth at the upcoming Singalong.

It wasn't a bad idea. They needed the money and some of the profit went to charity. Even so, she wasn't looking forward to asking Wilma about it!

As Belle was putting her coat on, her grandmother came into the hall with a plate of steaming hot toast covered in homemade strawberry jam. "Here you go, dear," she said as she handed it to her. "And here's your packed lunch. I put in some gingerbread for the drive too."

Belle smiled and took the plate of toast, tying her scarf around her neck as she did so. "Thanks Gram, you're the best! I'll eat breakfast on the way."

She kissed her on the cheek and headed out the door.

"I'll call Wilma and offer your hot chocolate booth for the Singalong for you," called Grace with a big smile as Belle opened her car door.

Belle nodded, and sighed with resignation.

Grace Beaumont had made up her mind, and Belle knew what that meant. It looked like she would have to set up her hot chocolate booth at the Christmas Singalong, whether she liked it or not.

No doubt, Wilma Figg would have something to say about that!

Chapter 7

Belle pulled back into the driveway after another successful day at the hot chocolate booth, and parked her car. Even though news had spread about the strange woman who had been found in the dumpster at the farm, people had still flocked to the farm to shop for Christmas trees. Belle had sold more hot chocolate that day than she had expected to.

I really need more comfortable shoes!

She looked at her worn boots. They were okay, but not good for standing in all day. Perhaps when she had saved up a little more money, she could afford to buy a new pair of shoes for Christmas.

Even though she was tired from a long day on her feet, Belle was looking forward to helping Grace and Doris with the gingerbread houses for the raffle.

She grabbed her bag and locked up the station wagon for the night, hurrying up the front steps. Stamping the snow from her boots, she unlocked the front door and called out a merry greeting.

"Gram? Doris? I'm home!"

Mittens ran to the door, meowing a welcome. He twined around Belle's legs, while she pulled her boots off and stacked them near the door. She pushed her feet into her slippers and picked up her cat, giving him a hug. Mittens rubbed his head against her chin and purred like a tractor.

"Hi, Belle! How was your day?" Grace called from the kitchen.

"It was busy," replied Belle, hanging up her coat on the rack. "We're going to have a good amount of money saved up soon, I think."

"Well, that's great," said Grace, as Belle entered the kitchen.

The two older women were sat at the kitchen table, working on two of the three gingerbread houses under construction. The shapes for the gingerbread houses were all cut out carefully and had been stuck together with piped icing. Doris was talking non-stop as she glued jellybeans onto white icing along the sides of the gingerbread, around the windows and around the doors. Chocolate buttons already formed a door knocker and covered the roof.

"And then you will never guess what they were saying down at the community center..." Doris was saying before she broke off and looked up. "Oh, hello Belle, dear."

Belle realized that Doris who had been industriously informing Grace of all the latest gossip from town. The woman was in her sixties, with a neat bun and glasses perched on her nose. Her eyes sparkled behind the glasses and she had a warm, welcoming smile.

"What have I missed?" asked Belle, as she washed her hands, ready to help decorate the second house.

Grace stood up and went to fetch more gingerbread. "You tell her Doris."

"We were just discussing that woman who died at Harvey's farm," said Doris as Belle sat down at the kitchen table. "No one knows who she was or what happened to her. Apparently, she didn't have a purse or identity documents on her at all. Did you know that they found a dead body at the farm where you work, Belle dear?"

"Yes, I was the one who found her," Belle said, with a serious expression. "In the dumpster."

"Oh, yes. I'd forgotten that. What a shock! You poor thing." She gave Belle a sympathetic pat on the hand. "Did you want to talk about it?"

Belle smiled ruefully at Doris' concern. "I'm all right, really. It *was* quite a shock though."

Doris tutted and shook her head. "It's all so strange. I don't think I can remember anything like that ever happening in Cherryville. And at Harvey's Christmas Farm, of all places! What do you think, my dear?" She turned to Belle's grandmother.

"Shocking, yes. But I suppose we'll never know," said Grace. "Especially if the police don't find anyone who knows her."

"It's a shame," said Doris, shaking her head in disbelief. "Not everyone visiting the Tree Farm is from Cherryville. There are visitors from all over the county. Out-of-towners. She could have been anyone."

Grace came back with the third gingerbread house on a plate and put it on the table in front of Belle as Doris continued telling them about the latest rumors.

Apparently, everyone in town had their own theory about who the woman was and how she had died. The theories ranged from being a runaway celebrity to being killed by Harvey for stealing a Christmas tree. Apparently, the local psychic was predicting that Harvey would be arrested before Christmas.

"Well, that's completely ridiculous," Belle exclaimed, as she put the finishing touches on the windows of the house. "Harvey wouldn't hurt anyone. He's such a teddy bear."

"Speaking of gossip," said Grace, as she balanced little coconut balls together to make a miniature snowman and stood it in front of the house that she was working on. "Wilma heard that Hollydale is going to have even more fireworks at their Singalong this year than we thought. You should have seen her face when she heard about that! She's anxious that our neighboring town may outdo us this year."

"Oh dear, that doesn't bode well," said Belle as she picked up the piping bag and outlined a chimney on the gingerbread house closest to her.

If there was anything that would put a bee in Wilma's bonnet, it would be Hollydale organizing a more spectacular Singalong than Cherryville.

"That's what I was thinking too," said Grace. "But Wilma is determined to have the best Singalong. She's going to have Harvey supply all the special lights for it. Even more than last year. She was telling me yesterday that she had also borrowed a television screen for the Singalong from the high school, so that we can display the words for the carols. We need people to help set everything up. One of her granddaughters has been told to prepare a slideshow with all the words for all the songs."

"Really?" Belle immediately felt sorry for Wilma's granddaughter.

Mittens meowed for his dinner and Belle scraped her chair back, heading to the pantry to prepare his favorite food.

"Don't people already know the words to the carols?" asked Grace as she worked on the side of her gingerbread house. "And if they don't remember the words, they can just read them from the little pamphlets that we bring out of storage every year. That's what we all bring our flashlights for."

"Oh no, that won't suit Wilma, I'm afraid. She doesn't want us to use those little pamphlets anymore. She wants everything on a big-screen television, like a concert. Wilma is determined to make it into a big spectacle and make sure that none of the folks from our town want to go to Hollydale for their Singalong," said Doris, shaking her head at Wilma's plans. "Plus, none of us are allowed to bring any flashlights this year."

"What?" Belle gasped as she stepped back out of the pantry. "But everyone uses their phones as flashlights these days. How is she going to stop us from using those? It's pitch black at night!" She quickly opened the cat food tin and emptied it into Mittens' bowl.

Doris shrugged. "She doesn't want any flashlights detracting from the look of all the Christmas lights that will be up around the old town market. I heard her saying that she wants everything so bright and cheerful that it will be visible from outer space. I hope she was speaking metaphorically."

"She can't outlaw flashlights," said Belle, decisively, placing the bowl of cat food on the floor. Mittens immediately started eating contentedly. "People will bring them anyway; people just do what they have always done."

"That's what I told Wilma too, but she wouldn't have any of it," said Doris, sounding exasperated. "She still wants the lights hung up on the trees along Main Street and around the square. I think it's going to be a bit too much this year." She finished the last of the piping around her gingerbread house with a flourish and stood back to admire her handiwork.

"I heard she's already told the local council to expect a drain on the electricity grid," commented Grace, as she glued a couple of peppermint candy canes on either side of a front door. "Wilma is certainly going overboard this year."

"Oh, dear," said Doris, rolling her eyes. She picked up a chocolate button and placed it on her gingerbread house roof. "I'm afraid it won't be long before she has us competing with Hollydale in everything. She even persuaded the Council to allow two pancake stands at the Singalong."

Grace perked up. "That reminds me, I was thinking..."

"Maybe it's better not to ask," interrupted Belle quickly, hoping to head off Gram's idea before she got too excited about it.

"... that we could get Belle to set up her hot chocolate booth at the Singalong," finished Grace, undeterred.

"Oh, that's a wonderful idea," Doris said, clapping her hands. "And a great way to raise funds for the charity."

"Oh, I don't know," Belle said with a dismissive shake of her head. "I'm sure Wilma won't be happy about it, not after Harvey declined her offer for the Women's Guild to run the hot chocolate booth at his Christmas Tree Farm this year. She had probably already made plans for the money that she was going to raise. And then he offered the booth to me instead. I'm not her favorite person right now."

"Belle doesn't want to risk upsetting Wilma," said Grace, widening her eyes. "Even for charity."

Belle put down her piping bag and gave her grandmother a stern look. "Well, all right, I'll do it then."

"That's my girl," said Grace, giving Belle a hug. "We'll tell her tomorrow night when we set up. Let's make her think that it's her idea. You leave Wilma to us."

"I would rather not upset Wilma," Belle agreed, not without some foreboding. "But you're right, we need to do what is best for the town and for charity."

"That's the spirit," Doris exclaimed as she looked at her watch. "Now I've got to go. My labrador will want his dinner."

Belle nodded, but she could not help privately worrying that things were about to get a lot more complicated in the run up to Christmas.

There was the hot chocolate booth to run, bills to pay, and the mystery of the dead woman to solve. And now her grandmother had talked her into helping out at the Singalong in the face of Wilma's likely disapproval. How on earth was she going to juggle it all?

Chapter 8

The next morning, Belle was up even earlier than normal. The events of the last few days had played on her mind all night again. She had only seen Harvey a few times the day before, as he had dashed about, anxiously filling large orders for Christmas trees.

Belle had tried to talk to him twice, but he had always seemed to be too busy to stop for a chat. She was getting increasingly worried about him. He was not being honest with the police or with her.

Knowing that she probably wouldn't be able to get back to sleep, Belle figured she might as well put the time to good use.

She rose, splashed some water on her face, then pulled on some fresh clothes, her stretchy denim pants and a chunky sweater, and headed downstairs.

Mittens heard her quietly getting ready for work and assumed that the only reason that she was awake was to make him breakfast and to switch on the heater for him. He padded downstairs and waited while she made toast for breakfast.

Belle put the kettle on the hob and, as soon as it started whistling, poured the boiling water over a spiced tea bag in a huge mug. She blew on it and sipped her tea, while shoving two slices of Grace's homemade bread into the toaster. The bread was soft and crisped up on the outside to a golden brown, just as she liked it. She smothered both slices of toast in butter and strawberry jam.

Mittens, who had been chomping away at his dish of cat food, looked up as Belle carried her breakfast to the breakfast table, then he followed her and sat nearby. Suddenly, he was much more interested in her toast than his cat food.

"Okay, Mittens my boy. Here you go." She broke off a piece of her toast and gave it to him. He licked it and then decided that this it was not as good as his cat food after all.

As she munched on her toast, Belle thought some more about the plan that had been formulating in her mind overnight.

She had to do something, and the only thing that she could think of was to see if Harvey had any documents in his office that could shed light on the woman that he had been arguing with.

Belle remembered his words. He had said "you agreed", or something to that effect. Perhaps that meant there was some sort of contract in his office. If she could find out what it was, and what he was hiding, perhaps she could help him. He had done so much for her and her grandmother, with the hot chocolate booth and everything.

Am I really contemplating breaking and entering?

She stared at her toast for a minute, then glanced up at the clock. It was five-thirty in the morning. No one would be up at the Christmas Tree Farm this early. Plus, Belle remembered seeing where Harvey had hidden the spare key to his office: under a plant pot at the side of the door. A plant pot with a little Christmas Tree in it.

If I use a key, technically it isn't breaking and entering, is it?

Having convinced herself that she needed to get into Harvey's office, Belle took a few minutes to devise a plan of action. It was a crazy idea, but it just might work. She was sure that she could find something in his office that would unravel the mystery.

She finished her breakfast and put the dishes in the dishwasher, then grabbed her handbag, keys, and phone, and the extra box of cocoa powder.

Mittens rushed to the front door, sat down and meowed.

"Sorry buddy, but I don't have time to take you for a walk this morning. You will need to use your litter box inside. Later, I promise. If Gram doesn't take you out first." She scribbled a note for her grandmother, grabbed her coat, and then quietly slipped out of the house.

The car was covered with snow again and Belle dusted the windscreen before climbing into the car. The drive to the tree farm took a mere twenty minutes. No one else in Cherryville was up and about, which suited Belle fine.

The sun was rising over the horizon as Belle swung into the parking lot of Harvey's Christmas Tree Farm. The only other vehicle in the lot was the expensive SUV that she had seen before. It was still covered in snow, like it had been there for a while. There were no trucks in the lot yet. They would probably still be in the road, heading in to collect a new stock of trees.

She glanced at the huge mound of snow in front of the entrance to the farm, right where the booth should be. The booth was barely visible. She would need a shovel to clear all of that snow away before she could set up for the day. But she didn't have time to worry about that now.

Belle locked up the car, pulled her faded blue coat tightly around her chest, and glanced around the parking lot to make sure that there was no one about. The early morning air was chilly and nipped at her nose, so she dashed across the open expanse of soft, new snow to Harvey's office. She knew that she was taking a risk, but she had to do something.

He had been so secretive about arguing with the now dead woman and it didn't feel right. If he had something to hide, then maybe she could help him. Maybe he would trust her enough to tell her the truth.

The tiny pot containing the miniature Christmas tree was exactly where she remembered. She felt around underneath it for the key, and when her fingers found the little piece of metal, she quickly opened the door, slipped inside the office, and shut the door behind her.

I'm in! Now what?

Belle's heart raced as she made her way across the office to Harvey's desk.

She gazed around her boss's office, marveling at how messy it was. There were papers everywhere, piled high in stacks on his desk and spilling onto the floor. Books and files were open all over his desk too.

It looked like a tornado had hit the place, but in the middle of all the chaos, she could see there was an order to it.

A method to his madness, as Gram would say.

She flipped through the papers on his desk, her eyes scanning them for anything that looked important. Most of the documents were invoices and bills, and copies of old sales and purchase agreements. There was also a lot of unopened mail strewn across the desk, but nothing that stood out.

It all looks so normal.

She sighed in frustration. What had she expected to find? If Harvey was in trouble, maybe he wouldn't leave something incriminating lying around in his office for anyone to find. What had she been thinking?

After several minutes, she had almost given up hope when she spotted a worn datebook on the edge of the desk, hidden beneath a mountain of pamphlets. She recognized it. Harvey often had it with him, pulling it out to scribble the occasional note, or to find someone's phone number. She grabbed the small book and flicked through the pages. It was full of appointments, notes and phone numbers. Belle felt a bit more hopeful. Maybe this was the key to solving the mystery.

She scanned through the pages until she found what she was looking for.

There, scribbled in the margin of a page, was a name: Victoria Dunn. The word "deadline" was scrawled underneath.

She looked at the date and time. Harvey had scheduled an appointment to meet Victoria Dunn at five o'clock. The same time and day that Belle had seen him arguing with the woman in the mulberry-colored coat.

"Who's Victoria Dunn?" Belle asked the empty office. "And what were you meeting her about?"

The datebook wasn't giving her any other clues. She flicked through the pages, searching for anything else that might help her work it out, but everything else was related to business. There were no personal entries at all.

Belle closed the datebook and stared at the cover, remembering how often she had seen Harvey take it with him wherever he went. He always seemed to consult it, jotting down notes in the margin when making calls from his office phone.

She was about to put it back on the desk when she noticed something odd. The corner of a small piece of paper tucked into the back of the book. The corner had a doodle of a heart on it. Belle pulled the piece of paper out and unfolded it. It was a receipt from a restaurant.

Belle's eyes widened. "The Spicy Olive! That's an expensive place!"

The Spicy Olive was a hotel restaurant in Hollydale. It served the most amazing food, but it was out of Belle's price range. She had only ever heard about it. The rooms of the hotel were, apparently, decorated in a Spanish style with expensive furnishings.

She quickly scanned through the receipt. The date was from a few weeks ago and the amount was for two hundred dollars! She couldn't believe it. Harvey had been to the Spicy Olive, and he had paid over two hundred dollars for dinner! That would be enough to buy a new pair of boots, and a fancy pair at that.

Belle's mind raced. What could Harvey have been doing at the Spicy Olive in Hollydale? And why was it worth spending that much money on one meal? She didn't know, but she could tell that there was something odd about this receipt and the doodle on it. He had saved it for a reason, and it wasn't for tax purposes, because it was the only loose piece of paper tucked into the back of the book.

She flipped the receipt over and noticed a name scribbled on it together with a phone number. Victoria.

"Victoria," she murmured to herself. "That must be the woman from the appointment in Harvey's datebook."

Had Harvey been meeting with Victoria Dunn to discuss something important? Something worth spending two hundred dollars on dinner for?

Belle was about to put the datebook back where she had found it when she heard a noise outside the office window. She ducked down behind Harvey's desk, heart pounding in her chest. She held her breath and listened.

The noise came again. It was the crunch of boots on snow. And they were coming closer to the office.

Chapter 9

Belle crouched lower and tried to make herself as small as possible. She had no idea who was outside, but she didn't want to get caught poking around Harvey's office this early in the morning.

Then she heard voices. It was Harvey! He called for Jerry, who answered back with his usual, "Yup?"

Belle's heart slowed down a bit. It sounded like Harvey was talking to Jerry like normal, and that there was no one else around. She poked her head up above the desk to get a better look through the window and saw them both walking toward the office.

Stuffing the datebook back under the pile of pamphlets, she rushed over to the single visitor's chair. She sat down, trying to appear like she had been there for a while. A little heater stood next to the chair. She flicked it on.

"Time for a morning coffee, eh Jerry?" Harvey said as they got closer to the office. "Did you bring some?"

"Sure thing, boss. It's back in the truck. Wife packed a large flask for us today," Jerry replied as he walked off.

Belle tried to keep her breathing steady and normal, as Harvey put his key in the door and found that it was already unlocked. He came in, looking surprised.

"I thought that I had locked that door last night. At least, I'm pretty that sure I did." He scratched his chin, looking confused.

Belle jumped up from the chair and immediately apologized for her early morning visit.

"Oh, my gosh! Harvey, I am so sorry!" she blurted out. "I was here early, and the booth was covered in so much snow that I needed help to shovel it. And it was too cold to wait in the car." She held out the spare key. "I remember you showing me where this was in case of emergencies."

"Oh, I see. Yeah, of course, no problem. It's too cold to wait outside," Harvey said with a smile. He switched on the light and walked over to his desk. "My office is a bit of a mess, I'm afraid."

Belle pretended to take in the surroundings. "Oh, it's not that bad," she lied. "You know, I could help you with your filing sometime if you want."

"Thanks, Belle. I may just take you up on that offer," Harvey said, as he picked up his datebook and shoved it in his pocket.

"So, at what crazy time did you get here?" he asked, looking around the room. "You must be the most dedicated of all of us."

Belle tried to play it cool. "Oh, I haven't been here all that long," she said, as casually as possible. She sat down on the edge of the visitor's chair and warmed her hands in front of the heater as it finally started blowing hot air. "I couldn't sleep, which is why I came in early. I kept thinking about that poor woman."

"Well, I'll be honest. I couldn't sleep either," Harvey said as he sat down across from Belle and started on some paperwork. "I was up all night worrying about what happened the other day. I hope you don't feel unsafe coming back to work. It's actually a good thing that you came into my office. I don't like to think of you here on your own after what has happened. Not until Sheriff Barnes figures it all out."

Now that she could see him more clearly, it looked like Harvey actually hadn't slept in several days. He was unshaven, and his eyes appeared haunted.

His words touched Belle. "I'm okay. I can manage." She smiled at him and turned her head to the side, as Jerry returned with his thermos flask. He closed the door against the cold and grabbed three canteen mugs from the filing cupboard before pouring steaming coffee into each of them.

"Here you go, boss," Jerry said as he handed Harvey a cup, then Belle one too.

She took it gratefully, inhaling the fresh coffee scent. Jerry's wife ran the diner in town and made great coffee.

"Thanks, Jerry," Harvey said, taking a sip of his coffee.

"So boss, have you heard anything more from the police about the investigation?" said Jerry conversationally. "The whole town is talking about it. Strange thing to happen around here. Like something you see on the news."

Belle pricked up her ears. Perhaps Harvey would say something about his argument with the woman who died. Victoria Dunn. That was the woman's name in Harvey's datebook. Belle tried to look as though she was concentrating on what Harvey was saying, but her mind was racing.

"I know Jerry, it's strange," Harvey said, leaning over the desk. "Terrible thing to have happened, and at my tree farm too! I just don't get it."

Trying not to look too eager, Belle asked the question that had been burning in her mind since she first saw the datebook. "Harvey, have you ever seen that woman before? The woman who died?"

Harvey hesitated. "No! Of course not." He raised his eyebrows. "Why would you ask that?"

"No one seems to know who she is. Or was," she said carefully, correcting herself. "She must have come from out of town."

"That's what the sheriff thinks too. He's trying to find out where she was staying." Harvey took a sip of coffee and looked thoughtful.

"What was she even doing here? She was clearly not from Cherryville. Was she here to buy a tree?" she asked, taking a sip of her own coffee.

"Dunno," Harvey said evasively, looking a little upset. "She just showed up at my tree farm. Dead."

Jerry leaned in closer too. "Do they know how she died yet?"

"The sheriff is still waiting on the autopsy report," Harvey said, grimacing. "But the rumor is that she was strangled. Why she was strangled on *my* farm I have no idea."

Belle tried to act casual as she asked her next question. "Is there anyone who would want to do you or your business any harm?"

"No! Of course not. At least I would hope not." Harvey looked around him as if to check that no one else could hear what they were saying.

Belle sat back in the visitor's chair, pretending that she was still warming her hands on the coffee mug. "Was there anyone who was angry with you? A customer perhaps?"

Jerry coughed. "She is right, boss. You know how it is. People get angry about the smallest things."

Harvey sighed and rubbed his temples. "I don't know, Belle. I have been racking my brain but I just can't think of anyone. We have our share of disgruntled customers, but nothing that would lead to this."

Belle contemplated what Harvey said. They were getting warmer. She needed to keep questioning him, and he might admit that he had some enemies after all.

She glanced at Jerry and nodded as if to say that he should keep going. But Jerry was a man of few words and just sipped his coffee, oblivious to Belle's encouragement to keep talking.

Outside, the sounds of the arriving trucks reverberated across the parking lot. Harvey was distracted for a moment as he looked outside.

"I better get going with the first orders." Harvey put his coffee down on the table.

"Do you think the killer could be someone from out of town? Maybe someone who was jealous of your business?" Belle tried to keep the impatience out of her voice. "It would have to be someone strong. Strong enough to lift her body into the dumpster."

"That's what the sheriff asked too. He's trying to find out how she ended up in that dumpster." Harvey looked thoughtful. "I still don't understand it. Why would someone kill her? It doesn't make any sense."

Jerry looked serious. "We need to be on the lookout in case whoever did this tries to harm someone else."

"Now you are scaring me, Jerry," Harvey said, shaking his head.

Jerry leaned back and gave a loud sigh. "I'm just trying to be realistic, boss. It's better to be safe than sorry."

Belle tried to look like she was thinking about what Jerry had said. In reality, she was trying to figure out a way to get Harvey alone, so she could ask him more questions about Victoria Dunn. She was sure that he was hiding something from her and she was determined to find out what it was.

The more she talked to Harvey, the more convinced she was that he had nothing to do with Victoria Dunn's death. He looked genuinely dumbfounded and disturbed by the events of the day before.

But he's hiding the fact that he knew Victoria Dunn. Why is that?

Belle excused herself to go to the lady's room, telling Harvey and Jerry that she needed to freshen up and get to work. She needed some time alone to think. She had a lot of questions, and she would need to be careful if she wanted to find out the truth without arousing suspicion.

Chapter 10

"Four jam doughnuts," said the young girl behind the counter of the diner, handing Belle a cardboard box.

Belle thanked her and handed over a couple of notes. The waitress tapped a few buttons on the register, extracted a couple of coins from the tray and handed Belle her change. "And the coffee takeout is on its way."

It was Saturday morning and Belle was taking the morning off from the hot chocolate booth to do the weekly grocery shopping, as well as attend to some chores in town. Plus, there was also somewhere in particular that she wanted to go. Most places opened a little later on Saturdays, including Harvey's Christmas Tree Farm. Harvey had said that she could open her booth after lunch. The tree farm stayed open later on Saturdays anyway.

The diner was getting ready for the lunchtime crowd, even though it was not yet ten o'clock in the morning. The smell of frying onions and bacon made her stomach growl. But she had a job to do first.

Within a couple of minutes, the coffee that she had ordered was ready too. Two cups of the best coffee in town. She hoped that, together with the doughnuts, it would be enough to get the sheriff talking.

Balancing the box of doughnuts and the cardboard tray holding the coffee cups, Belle shouldered the door open and headed to the police station.

She was pleased to see that Sheriff Barnes was in his office and was on the phone. He waved her in and pointed to the chair on the other side of his desk. Belle put the cups and doughnuts down on the edge of the desk and sat down, waiting for the sheriff to finish his call.

"I'll see you later then, Harry," said Sheriff Barnes into the phone. "Thanks for calling." He hung up.

Belle opened the box and offered him a doughnut.

"Well, this is nice," said the sheriff with a friendly smile. "What's the occasion?"

"No occasion." Belle shrugged. "I just brought some coffee and doughnuts to Cherryville's finest. Thought I would stop by and say hi. Don't tell my grandmother that I paid for store-bought doughnuts or she will insist on making three dozen of them herself."

The sheriff chuckled. He picked up a doughnut and took a bite. "Well, that won't be such a bad thing. Mmm, these are good."

Belle sat back and watched as the sheriff devoured his doughnut. Then she took a sip of her coffee. It was hot and strong, just the way she liked it.

"So, what can I do for you?" said the sheriff when he had finished his doughnut. "Are you here about the dead woman?"

Belle nodded. "I was hoping that you might tell me more about her. It's worrying, what with me working at the hot chocolate booth there and all."

The sheriff leaned back in his chair and steepled his fingers. "What would you like to know?"

Belle took a deep breath. "Well, for starters, can you tell me her name? Have you figured out who she is?"

The sheriff nodded. "Yes, we've identified the victim. I guess it's okay to tell you; we will do a press release shortly. Her name is Victoria Dunn."

Victoria Dunn! Belle's eyes widened.

The name that she had seen in Harvey's datebook. So, she was right! She was the woman that Harvey had been arguing with a few days ago.

"Did she live in town? I don't recognize that name."

The sheriff shook his head. "No, she was from Hollydale. We have notified her husband. The poor man is quite heartbroken."

Belle took a sip of her coffee and then grabbed another doughnut. This was getting complicated. The woman had a husband! "I heard that she was strangled."

"Yes, that's right," said the sheriff, with a serious expression. "With the rope of tinsel that we found with her. And then dumped in the dumpster."

"That's awful," said Belle, her heart sinking. She steeled herself. She had to be honest with the sheriff. "Sheriff, I have to tell you that a piece of tinsel went missing from my booth. I was wondering if it was the same piece that was found with that poor woman."

The sheriff nodded grimly. "We thought it was a possibility when we saw all the decorations that you had up," he said. "But it could also have been taken from the stock of decorations that Harvey has for sale at the farm."

Belle didn't know whether to be relieved about the sheriff's comment or not.

"Do you have any idea why someone would want to kill her?"

The sheriff shook his head again. "That's what we haven't been able to figure out. And we don't know why she was at the tree farm at all. But we're doing our best to find out. Unfortunately, we don't have much to go on."

Belle sighed and leaned back in the chair. This was harder than she had thought. If she was going to help Harvey, she needed to find out more information about Victoria Dunn.

"Did *you* see anything that could help?" said the sheriff. "Anything that you can remember? There were no real clues at the scene of the crime. And if there were, the snow obliterated them."

Belle sat up straight and took a deep breath. She didn't want to make Harvey look bad in front of the sheriff, but she wanted him to find Victoria's murderer. Before she told the sheriff that she saw the woman arguing with Harvey, she needed to figure out why Harvey had lied about knowing Victoria.

But she could help the sheriff out with something else.

"Well, she was wearing the most expensive coat that I have ever seen. It was a real designer coat. Made by Gaultier or something like that."

The sheriff's brows shot up. "Really?" he asked. "And how do you know that? Did you see the label?"

Belle shook her head. "No, but I remember seeing that style in one of Doris's fashion magazines. And when I touched it...." She shuddered briefly at the memory. "To wake her up, you know... the fabric felt expensive. Like it was made of cashmere or something. It must have cost a lot of money."

The sheriff nodded and made a note on his desk. "That's helpful," he said. "Thanks for telling me that." He looked thoughtful for a moment. "The lady obviously had a lot of money. Which is strange."

Belle looked surprised. "Why do you say that?"

The sheriff smiled slightly. "Well, we put her name through our database to check for any outstanding warrants and such. She had no criminal record. She didn't even have a parking ticket. But something else came up."

Belle leaned forward. "What's that?"

"There were a lot of debt collectors looking for her."

Belle's ears pricked up.

So, Victoria Dunn was in debt! Maybe she was a compulsive spender.

"Well, if I bought a coat like the one that she was wearing, I would be in a lot of debt too," commented Belle before she could stop herself.

The sheriff chuckled. "I guess you would."

Belle shifted in her seat. "So, what about the other people working at the tree farm? Do you think anyone else might be in danger?" she asked, trying to change the subject.

The sheriff shrugged. "We don't know right now." He took another sip of his coffee. "But we want everyone to be careful. Until we figure all of this out, we just don't want anything else to happen. Bad enough that we're dealing with such an incident just before Christmas as it is."

Belle nodded her head. "I'll be careful."

Sheriff Barnes reached out for another doughnut and took a bite. He patted his stomach. "I know I shouldn't, and I hate to be a cliché, but these are too good." He smiled at her. "Thanks for bringing them by."

Belle smiled and took another sip of her coffee. She had helped the sheriff out and now she could focus on figuring out what was going on with Harvey. It made her feel less guilty about not telling Sheriff Barnes everything that she knew.

After a bit of chitchat, Belle took her leave and headed back to her car. She had to swing by the grocery store before she went home and she had a lot of thinking to do.

What had Victoria Dunn been doing at Harvey's Christmas Tree Farm?

Although there were a few customers who travelled from afar to buy Harvey's excellent trees, they were usually distributors who bought several trees wholesale. A few families came to the farm every year because they made a tradition out of taking a fun road trip before Christmas to fetch a tree. Quite a few florists visited every year too. They liked to buy large stocks of trees for pre-orders before Christmas.

Victoria Dunn hadn't looked like any of those kinds of people.

She didn't look like she would have driven all the way from out of town to buy a Christmas tree. She looked like she had money. Like she was someone who would pay a decorator to install a tree and do all the work for her. She didn't look like a person who would buy a Christmas tree wholesale. But then she had been in serious debt, so maybe she had no money for fancy decorators after all, and had come to pick up a tree like everyone else.

So, what was she doing arguing with Harvey three days ago?

"Well, I guess Sheriff Barnes will have to find out," said Belle to herself as she inched the car into a parking spot at the grocery store. "We're just going to have to wait and see what he comes up with."

But she couldn't help but feel that the Sheriff didn't have many leads to go on. He had mentioned that there were no further clues at the scene of the crime. The snow had hidden the murderer's tracks, and there were no eyewitnesses.

Belle thought about the restaurant receipt which she had seen in Harvey's datebook. The Spicy Olive. That was the hotel restaurant over in Hollydale.

Perhaps it wasn't the first time that Harvey and Victoria had argued.

She shivered as she thought about what it could mean for Harvey.

It was looking more and more like her kind boss had become involved in something that he shouldn't be mixed up in. In fact, if Belle could hazard a guess, she thought that Harvey really needed someone in his corner right about now.

Chapter 11

Smithy's Grocery, in the center of town, was where everyone went to get their groceries. It was a small, independent store that offered a little of everything.

Right now, it was flooded with people stocking up for the Christmas season. The place was packed, not only with people, but with new stock for the holidays. There were hams, turkeys, piles of fresh vegetables, boxes of Christmas crackers, and every kind of chocolate imaginable. Festive streamers and tinsel adorned the aisles, and even the cash registers were wearing little Santa hats.

Belle grabbed a shopping cart and headed down the first aisle. The little wheels of the cart squeaked along the checked linoleum to the Christmas music that drifted out of the store's sound system.

Belle hummed to herself as she filled her cart with goodies. With her weekly wages, she had some money to spend. Besides the usual staples, Belle splashed out and selected a bottle of Cook's sherry. It was expensive, but she decided that it was worth it for the occasion. Plus, she knew that her grandmother loved to cook with sherry. She also got Mittens some cat treats and a new collar for Christmas.

The store was busier than she had seen it in a long time, with shoppers navigating their carts past each other, piled high with Christmas supplies. Belle held her cart tightly, trying to keep track of everything that she put in it.

As Belle stood in line for the check-out, she waited behind a few of the women from town. One of them was speaking to the lady working the cash register, Mrs. Haggerty.

"It's such a tragedy, isn't it? Poor woman. I heard that she was smothered and hidden in a dumpster up at Harvey's Christmas Tree Farm." The woman crossed her arms as if ready to talk for some time.

Belle's heart jumped into her throat. She had to hold on to her shopping cart for support.

"That's what I heard too," Mrs. Haggerty replied. "Tragic."

"Only seen her in the store once before. Apparently, she was some rich lady from out of town," said the customer in the front of the line. "My friend who lives over in Hollydale said that her name is Mrs. Dunn. Not sure of her first name though."

Mrs. Haggerty looked around the store, as though she was worried that someone might be listening. "I shouldn't be telling you this, but I heard from my cousin at the bank that some sizeable sums of money were transferred to Mrs. Dunn's bank account from Harvey's bank account. About six months ago. Next thing you know, the woman turns up dead. On his farm, of all places!"

The other woman gasped. "Was Harvey in business with her?"

"Well, it's not for me to say," said Mrs. Haggerty. "But I wouldn't be surprised if the police are looking into his finances."

Belle's stomach turned over.

Harvey gave Victoria money?

"I don't know, but something fishy is going on, that's for sure," Mrs. Haggerty said. "My cousin at the bank had to call Harvey. You know, to get authorization for the transfer to Mrs. Dunn's account." She lowered her voice dramatically. "Apparently, he said it was okay and also that the money would be transferred back into Harvey's bank account on the fifteenth of December."

Belle felt faint. That was the same day Victoria died.

"Oh, my!" the customer said, putting her hand over her mouth in shock. "That can only mean one thing. She must have been blackmailing him."

"I know, right?" said Mrs. Haggerty grimly. "But what could she possibly have been blackmailing him about?"

The other customer shook her head. "I'm sure we'll find out sooner or later. It's all anyone is talking about at the moment."

Blackmail? Surely not.

In all the time that Belle had known Harvey, he had been nothing but an upstanding citizen. He helped at the local soup kitchen and he was always willing to lend a hand to anyone. The woman's comments about blackmail were pure gossip, surely.

But if what she had overheard was true, Harvey had lent Victoria money. Why he would do so was a mystery. He must have given it to her on the belief that she would repay him by the fifteenth of December—the same day that she had died! But then, Sheriff Barnes had said that Victoria had left enormous debts.

The conversation at the cash register interrupted Belle's musings.

"... and maybe that's why he killed her?" the woman in the line was saying.

Mrs. Haggerty shrugged. "Who knows? The police are investigating; it's all so mysterious. I just hope that they catch the killer before Christmas. We can't have a mad killer on the loose. Not with the Singalong coming up and everything."

"I would never have thought that Harvey could kill someone," piped up the woman's friend.

Mrs. Haggerty shook her head. "Me neither. But you never know what someone is capable of. You see this kind of stuff on the TV all the time. People get interviewed about living next door to a murderer, and all the time they never knew. That could be us, you know."

"I wonder if they will send television crews here," replied the other woman, perking up. "We could all be on TV soon."

Belle stood in shock. She was still processing what she had just heard. Harvey had lent Victoria money six months ago, which was supposed to be repaid to him the night Victoria died. Clearly, she didn't have the money because, according to Sheriff Barnes, the woman was up to her eyeballs in debt. Could Harvey have killed Victoria because she couldn't pay him back? Surely not. The thought made Belle's stomach churn. She didn't know what to do—should she go back to Sheriff Barnes and tell him about the argument that she had overheard on the night of the murder? But what if she was wrong and Harvey was innocent? She didn't know who to believe anymore.

When Belle finally reached the cash register, she lifted her groceries out of the cart and onto the counter, her mind in turmoil. She couldn't get the image of Victoria's dead body out of her head. And even though she wanted to trust Harvey, his secret loan was suspicious.

Plus, his secret loan wasn't much of a secret anymore. It seemed like the whole town was talking about it. That didn't bode well for Harvey's future in the town, or for his business.

"Oh honey, it's you," said Mrs. Haggerty as she recognized Belle. "How's your booth going?" She leaned forward, eager to add to her stock of gossip. "I heard it was you who found the body." She fixed Belle with a beady look.

Belle gave her a smile. "Yes, the booth is going well. Thank you for the extra order of cocoa," she said, referring to the cocoa that Mrs. Haggerty had ordered from the supplier for her the previous week.

"Must have given you quite a turn to see a dead body, my dear," said Mrs. Haggerty, single-mindedly focused on the most recent rumors and prompting her for information. She watched Belle closely.

Belle looked around at the line of interested customers gazing at her and thought about Harvey and his kindness. He really didn't deserve to be fodder for the town gossip mill. "I really didn't see all that much," she said evasively. "It was all a bit of a blur."

"That's to be expected, dear," said Mrs. Haggerty, sympathetically. "You've been through a lot. Now, what do you think of Harvey?" She lowered her voice conspiratorially.

Belle frowned. "He's been really kind to me. I think we should all give him the benefit of the doubt."

Mrs. Haggerty tutted. "You're too trusting. Myself, I don't trust him as far as I can throw him."

Mrs. Haggerty's words took Belle aback. She didn't want to believe that her boss could be capable of murder.

"I think you should stay away from him, dear." Mrs. Haggerty raised her brows at the look of doubt on Belle's face. "It's not safe. I know you're in charge of Wilma's old booth and want to make a success of it. But perhaps you should set it up elsewhere. I could call in some favors if you need. You could set up near the scout hall, perhaps."

"Thank you for the offer," Belle said politely, "but I'm going to stay and see this through. I think we should all be helping Harvey."

Mrs. Haggerty gave her a doubtful look, but said no more.

Belle finished loading her groceries into her cart, paid for them, and then headed out to the car lot. It was a short drive home, and her mind was reeling. She still couldn't believe that Harvey could be guilty of murder, but the circumstances weren't looking good.

And the money that Harvey had lent to Victoria? The sheriff had said that debt collectors were looking for her. That meant she clearly did not have the money to pay Harvey back on the day that his loan was due to be repaid. Which was the same day that Victoria had been killed. Could that have been the motive for murder?

There was only one way to find out the truth. She would have to talk to Harvey.

Chapter 12

Monday dawned with the clear winter sky that made the postcards at the Cherryville post office look so picturesque. Belle was about to head out to the hot chocolate booth, early as usual.

"Here you go, my dear," said Grace, handing her a packed lunch. "I made you a thermos of caramel-flavored coffee too. I know that it's your favorite. And there's a cinnamon roll for morning tea, freshly baked. And then a turkey sandwich with cranberry sauce."

When she heard about the cinnamon roll, a little thrill of anticipation ran through Belle. Caramel-flavored coffee was indeed her favorite and there was nothing better than Gram's turkey sandwiches.

"Thanks!" she exclaimed with genuine appreciation.

"You're welcome," Grace smiled. "Now, be careful out there. Don't work too hard."

Mittens meowed for attention as she gave him a quick pat on the head. "I'll be back soon, I promise."

The sun was just peeking over the horizon, casting a pink and orange glow through the window.

The drive to the tree farm was becoming more familiar, like an old friend that she could always rely on. Before she knew it, Belle was pulling into the lot and parking her station wagon in the usual spot.

The lot was gradually filling up with the usual delivery trucks. However, there was something different about this morning. She looked around frowning, before realizing what had changed. The expensive-looking SUV was gone. The car that had been parked in the lot for the last few days.

She had planned to use the commute to think. How was she going to ask Harvey about Victoria? How did someone ask about something that they weren't supposed to see?

Maybe I should just tell him that I saw him talking to Victoria last week. Before I found the poor woman dead. But then he may ask why I didn't tell the police!

Also, it was awkward to tell Harvey that people were talking about his money transactions at the grocery store, thanks to old Mrs. Haggerty's contacts at the bank.

She sighed and got out of the car, grabbing her thermos and lunch bag. Talking to Harvey was going to be more difficult than she had thought.

The booth looked more or less as she had left it on Saturday. Fortunately, less snow had fallen overnight, so it wouldn't need much clearing.

Putting her worries about Harvey out of her mind for a little while, Belle got busy setting up her booth, carrying the Christmas decorations from her car and hanging the lights over the little canopy above the counter. She plugged in the extension cable to the power outlet near Harvey's office and ran the cable along the path. In no time, she had the hot chocolate Crock-Pot heating. She opened another packet of cocoa and a box of sugar and added the ingredients to the pot, stirring in the spices.

The smell of cinnamon and sugar soon wafted through the air, picking up her spirits and Belle feel more cheerful. The first few Christmas tree customers trickled in, rubbing their hands together, their breath fogging in the cold air.

"Merry Christmas!" she greeted them as they came up to the booth. "Would you like a cup of hot chocolate?"

"Oh yes, please," said one woman as she pulled out some bills. Her companion stood next to her, stamping his feet on the ground to stay warm.

Belle turned to grab two cups from the stack on the shelf behind her. She prepared two steaming cups of her special hot chocolate recipe, complete with bobbing marshmallows, and handed them over.

"Merry Christmas!" she said again as they took their drinks and walked away to inspect a nearby pine tree.

As the morning wore on, more customers came through the tree farm, the line in front of Belle's booth growing longer by the minute.

"Merry Christmas," she said cheerfully, as she handed out cups of hot chocolate. More than once, customers asked if she would have any left for when they returned from choosing their tree. She couldn't imagine that there would be people shopping for trees for that long, but then again, the farm was huge. It took a while to walk around and look at all the stock. And some people were very particular when choosing their perfect Christmas tree. It was no wonder people wanted more than one hot drink.

During a brief lull in customers, Belle grabbed her thermos of coffee and her cinnamon roll. She took a big bite and was savoring the sweet and sticky goodness when a familiar voice suddenly spoke behind her.

"How are you holding up?"

Belle jumped and turned around to see Harvey standing there, a box of Christmas lights in his arms. He wore a woolen hat over his balding head.

"I'm good, thanks," she said thickly, through a mouthful of cinnamon roll. "How are you?"

He pulled a face. "As well as expected, I see you're busy, like always."

"Yes, I am. It's been a little busier today than yesterday. But that's probably because it's Monday and five days before Christmas."

There was an awkward pause, and then Harvey cleared his throat. "Listen, I wanted to talk to you about something."

Belle held her breath. Was he going to finally admit that he knew Victoria Dunn? He must have a good reason for not telling the police about that.

"What is it?"

Harvey shifted his weight from one foot to the other, looking a little uncomfortable. "I may face some financial difficulties soon, and so I can't offer you a job after the holidays. You remember that we spoke the other day about you possibly helping with my filing?"

Belle had forgotten, but tried not to let it show. "Yes, I remember."

"Well, the thing is," Harvey continued, "I can only pay you for running this booth until Christmas. After that, I won't be able to afford to pay you anything."

"I see."

"Don't worry, I wouldn't ask you to work for free," Harvey said quickly. "I know you're hardworking. I've seen that already. And I'll do whatever I can to help you get a job with anyone else."

Belle took the opportunity as it presented itself. "Are you having difficulties because of Victoria Dunn?" she asked bluntly.

Harvey looked taken aback. "What?"

"Have you got financial troubles because of Victoria Dunn? Did she owe you money?"

Harvey's face had gone very pale. "How did you find out about that?" His voice sounded strangled.

"You were arguing with her the other day," Belle blurted out, unable to stop herself. "Then Sheriff Barnes said that Victoria Dunn was heavily in debt."

Harvey nodded and winced. "I had hoped that nobody had heard us arguing."

"I'm sorry, but I did," she said simply. "I have not told the sheriff yet. Why don't you tell me what happened?"

Harvey sighed and ran a hand through his hair. "Victoria owed me a lot of money. She was going to pay me back a few days ago. But she didn't have it. That's what we were arguing about."

"And then...?" Belle prompted gently.

"Well, we argued. I told her she shouldn't have come to the tree farm. Then she left. That was the last time that I saw her and then...," he replied, his voice still sounding strained.

"And then I found her in the dumpster," Belle completed the sentence for him.

Harvey nodded; his face creased with concern. "Yes, that's right. I should never have lent her the money, but I felt sorry for her."

Belle looked at Harvey, trying to gauge his reaction. He seemed to be telling the truth, but she still wasn't sure. "Why didn't you tell the Sheriff this?"

Pride flickered across his face. "I didn't think it was relevant. Plus, I didn't want everyone in Cherryville to know about me lending money to her."

Belle crossed her arms over her chest. "I'm not so sure. It seems to me like it may be relevant. Plus, you know Cherryville, no secret is safe here. How much money did she borrow?"

Harvey ran a hand through his hair again. "Yes, you're right." He sighed. "It was a lot. Nearly half of what this farm is worth. First, it was a little and then she kept asking for more. She said she would pay off her debts a few months ago and then promised to pay me back on the fifteenth of December. But when the day arrived and she was supposed to bring the money in cash, she turned up with weak excuses. Said that she had never agreed to pay me back that day. It has put me in quite a bit of financial difficulty, to be honest. But I didn't kill Victoria. I swear it. I wouldn't do that to anybody."

The poor man looked so wretched that Belle couldn't help but feel sorry for him. "I believe you. And I think that you need to tell Sheriff Barnes the truth."

He let out a breath and gave her a weak smile. "Thank you," he said. "I appreciate it. I'll tell him about arguing with Victoria over the loan."

"And we need to figure out who did this before it happens again. Sheriff Barnes doesn't have many leads. Someone who was at the tree farm killed Victoria. Perhaps the murderer also overheard you arguing with her. Can you think of anyone who would want to cause Victoria harm?"

"No," Harvey said, shaking his head. "I really can't."

Belle was quiet for a moment, trying to think of anyone who may have had a motive. It occurred to her that Harvey gave jobs to ex-convicts to give them a chance in life. "Maybe it's somebody you hired? Somebody with a criminal record?"

Harvey shook his head again. "I doubt it. Most of the ex-cons that I hire have a criminal record, but not for committing violent crimes like murdering someone."

"Well, do you know if Victoria borrowed money from anyone else?" Belle crossed her arms and paced back and forth. "If she needed money from you and couldn't pay it back, then perhaps she borrowed money from someone else. There are some unscrupulous loan sharks out there, and they can be quite dangerous."

Harvey thought for a moment. "She hadn't. She promised me that she hadn't. I wouldn't have loaned her money otherwise. I wanted her to pay her original debts. She promised that she wouldn't use it to pay back unscrupulous loan sharks."

Belle sighed in frustration. She was no closer to finding out who killed Victoria than she was before this conversation! But at least Harvey had agreed to tell the sheriff the truth. And that was a start.

Chapter 13

Harvey left to take the box of Christmas lights to one of the trucks and Belle turned her attention back to the booth.

There were fewer customers arriving now. The morning flurry of activity was over. Most of the early morning deliveries had been picked up already, and only the occasional out-of-towners came through.

Belle stirred the Crock-Pot of chocolate, sprinkled in some freshly grated nutmeg, and then replaced the lid. She had sold the morning's batch and had only a few cups left. Checking on the marshmallow levels, she made a mental note to order some more from Mrs. Haggerty at the grocery store. Adding extra marshmallows to everyone's cups meant that she was getting through them faster than expected.

Her mind drifted back to her conversation with Harvey. She felt better now that she had spoken with him. She had to believe that he was innocent. The poor man had looked so worried about everything, and now he was in financial difficulties because he had generously lent money to a woman in an expensive coat who couldn't—or wouldn't—repay him. He didn't deserve this. And he didn't deserve all of the town gossiping about him either. It could destroy his business. The Christmas Tree Farm was his life, and he had worked so hard on it.

Between serving customers steaming cups of hot chocolate, Belle tried to come up with a plan. She had to do something. But what could she do?

While she was racking her brain, a truck driver ambled over to the booth and asked for a cup. He put some coins on the counter. She realized that he was the same tall, thin guy who had come with Jerry when they discovered the body in the dumpster. He didn't smile much.

"Merry Christmas," said Belle politely. "What will it be? A large or an extra-large?"

"Extra-large," replied the man shortly.

Belle wondered if he was an ex-con, and if he was the type of criminal who wouldn't think twice about murdering someone. He certainly looked unfriendly and strong enough to lift another person, with his biceps bulging through his checked shirt. Belle glanced sideways at the man and tried not to let her thoughts show on her face as she prepared his cup of hot chocolate.

Just then, a police car cruised into the tree farm car park and came to a halt, its tires crunching on the churned-up snow. The lights of the police car were flashing, although the siren wasn't blaring.

Sheriff Barnes climbed out, pushing the car door closed in a business-like way. When he turned to face Belle, his face was stern.

"Good morning, Belle. I need to speak with Harvey. Have you seen him today?"

Belle's heart sank. She could tell that it wasn't good news. The sheriff had that look about him, like he wouldn't be taking no for an answer.

The truck driver spoke up. "Yes, officer. The boss is in his office." He pointed up the hill to the pre-fabricated building that served as Harvey's office. "He was just helping me with a bulk order a minute ago."

The sheriff nodded. "Thanks for that."

Belle's pulse quickened.

She watched as the sheriff made his way up to Harvey's office and headed out of view. She stood for a few minutes, undecided about what to do. Then, she hastily handed the truck driver his cup of hot chocolate and dashed up the hill to Harvey's office.

The door was open as she walked around the side of the office. The policeman stood on the stairs, talking to Harvey.

She heard the sheriff say, ".... proof that you and Victoria were in a romantic relationship."

Belle's heart lurched.

A romantic relationship? Surely, that couldn't be right?

Victoria Dunn was married and wore expensive clothes, while Harvey was a down-to-earth guy in a plaid shirt and jeans.

Belle stepped forward. "Is there a problem, Sheriff?"

The sheriff turned to face her. "I'm afraid so, Belle. We have evidence that Harvey was having an affair with Victoria Dunn." The policeman turned back to Harvey. "And all evidence of her murder points to you. Harvey, you're under arrest for the murder of Victoria Dunn."

Belle's mouth fell open, and all she could do was stare at Harvey.

The man's face was ashen, and he looked like he was about to pass out. He swayed on his feet and the policeman had to grab him to stop him from falling.

"What?" Belle gasped. "Harvey couldn't have done that! He's innocent!"

The sheriff gave her a grim stare, then turned back to Harvey, who still stood on the steps outside his office, supported by the policeman. "We understand that Harvey loaned Victoria a lot of money. Money that she was due to pay him on the day that she was killed. Right here, on Harvey's premises. That's hardly a coincidence. Especially now that we know they were in a secret romantic relationship."

Belle shook her head. "No, it's not. But there must be another explanation."

The sheriff sighed. "I'm sorry, Belle, but it doesn't look good. We have enough evidence to charge him with Victoria Dunn's murder and take him in for questioning."

Belle couldn't take her eyes off of her boss. He looked like a broken man.

"But maybe you could... I don't know..." Belle's voice trailed off as she thought about what Sheriff Barnes said.

Harvey had been dating Victoria!

The sheriff fixed her with a steely gaze. "Belle, you're going to have to come with me too, if you continue to interfere."

"It's okay, Belle," said Harvey, in a kindly way, his voice low. "I deserve it, I'm sure."

"You have the right to remain silent," said the sheriff sternly as he fastened a pair of handcuffs around Harvey's wrists. "Anything you say can and will be used against you in a court of law."

Harvey's gaze flicked from Belle to Sheriff Barnes, and an expression of resignation settled on his face.

By now, a few of the men that helped Harvey out on the farm, digging up the Christmas trees and loading them onto the trucks, had heard their raised voices. They gathered near Harvey's office, all looking at the scene with worried expressions.

"What's going on, boss?" asked Jerry. "Are you in some kind of trouble?"

"He sure is," said Sheriff Barnes grimly. "Harvey is under arrest for the murder of Victoria Dunn, a woman that he had an affair with."

The men all looked shocked.

"You can't do that!" Jerry's round face frowned in anger. "Boss didn't do any such thing."

"It's true Jerry. Belle," said Harvey, with resignation. "I had an affair with Victoria. I even loaned her money. But it didn't last long. I broke it off with her when I found out that she was married. She said that she would leave her husband, but then she said a lot of things. I definitely didn't kill her though."

"Better not say anything more until you have a lawyer with you," said Jerry stoutly, glancing at Sheriff Barnes. He caught Harvey's eye and gave him a reassuring nod. "I'll call my brother-in-law. He's a lawyer. He'll help you out."

The other men nodded.

Sheriff Barnes nodded. "Do what you need to do. I'll take Harvey down to the station now and ask him some questions. If he's done nothing wrong, then he doesn't need to be worried. However, if Victoria Dunn's blood is on his hands, then he will go to jail."

He led Harvey down to the car park and helped him into the back seat of the police car, as Belle and the men watched.

Jerry called out reassurance to Harvey again. "I'll get my brother-in-law to the police station as soon as possible, Harvey. Just hang in there."

Belle felt a sense of panic as she watched the police car drive away, with Harvey in the back.

"What are we going to do, Jerry?" she asked the older man.

The others dispersed, whispering amongst themselves.

"We have to help the boss, Belle. Harvey has done so much for all of us. We have to find out who really killed Victoria Dunn and put them behind bars." The farmhand stamped his feet in the snow and pulled his hat down over his head. "Now, if you will excuse me, I'm going to find me a lawyer!"

Belle nodded and smiled gratefully. "Thanks, Jerry. That's just what I was hoping you would say. What can I do?"

"Not much at the moment, other than keeping Harvey's business running while he is gone." Jerry rubbed his calloused hands together. "Keep selling your hot chocolate and keep the customers happy."

Since she didn't know what else to do, Belle continued to do just that. She worked at the hot chocolate booth until just after five o'clock, then packed up for the day. There was a lot to think about. Sheriff Barnes had said that they had enough evidence to convict Harvey of Victoria's murder. But Belle couldn't believe that it was true. There must be another explanation. She would have to find out what really happened, and fast.

But how?

Since no one in town knew Victoria, the most obvious thing to do would be to travel to where Victoria lived and ask about her there. But who would know anything about the woman who had come to Harvey's Christmas Tree Farm uninvited?

As she wiped down the counter of the booth and switched the Crock-Pot off, Belle tried to think of the most likely people who would know about Victoria's financial problems. There was one other person who Belle could think of that may know about Victoria's debts.

Sheriff Barnes had said that Victoria was married.

Perhaps Mr. Dunn, whoever he was, would know if Victoria had borrowed money from someone else. A loan shark, perhaps.

Having decided to talk to Victoria's husband, Belle packed up the booth quickly and drove back to her grandmother's house.

She would find out what really happened to Victoria Dunn and clear Harvey's name, no matter what it took.

Chapter 14

"What? Harvey's been arrested?" exclaimed Grace.

Belle sighed. "Yes. For the murder of that woman that I found on his farm. Victoria Dunn from Hollydale." Belle had filled her grandmother in on everything that had happened that day.

"Good heavens," said Grace, her face paling. "Poor Harvey. I can't believe it. I'm sure that no one would ever think that he would do something like this."

Belle shook her head, worry etched on her face. "I don't know. But he will clear his name soon, won't he? I am sure that he is innocent."

"Of course, he is," said Grace adamantly. "No one in *our* town could be so wicked as to kill someone. It will all work out, Belle. You'll see."

"I wonder if her husband knows anything that could help. You know, about who she may have borrowed money from?"

Grace frowned. "Best leave it to Sheriff Barnes, my dear. Anyway, you can't do anything to help Harvey this evening. We need to get to the old town market square to help set everything up for tomorrow's Singalong," she said. "Tomorrow is the big day."

While Belle felt better after talking to her grandmother, she really did not feel up to an evening of setting up Christmas decorations in the center of town.

"With everything that's going on, maybe it is not the best idea for us to hold the Singalong," said Belle, still a little anxious. "Harvey was supposed to oversee the installation of the gigantic Christmas tree, but he can't at the moment because he's in the county lockup. Plus, he supplied all of the Christmas lights that we're setting up, and many of the people in town may not be too happy with him right now."

"Nonsense. We're going. It will be fun, and we have a lot of work to do tonight. We can't just abandon our neighbors because of this. Harvey wouldn't want us to."

Belle could see the determination in her grandmother's eyes and knew there was no point in arguing with her. She would have to help out tonight and figure out how to help Harvey tomorrow.

Leaving Mittens curled up in his favorite cat bed, they headed into town. Grace had packed some of her freshly baked shortbread cookies for the volunteers setting up for the Singalong and the fresh scent of vanilla filled the car. It was fortunately not snowing, but Belle still parked as close to the square as she could.

The old town market was a large open space surrounded by old red brick buildings that were now converted into shops and cafés. Overhead, strings of fairy lights were strung from building to building, and a large Christmas tree was already hoisted into place in the middle of the square. Boxes of silver and gold decorations were stacked nearby, ready to be hung on the tree once all the lights were up.

Grace immediately spotted Jerry from the tree farm, supervising the setting up of the tree, together with some of the other men that helped Harvey dig up the trees and load up the trucks.

"Hello Jerry," said Grace as they walked up. "Belle told me that Harvey has been arrested. I'm so sorry."

Jerry shook his head. "It's terrible. I can't believe that this has happened to him. But we'll get through it. The tree is going up, even without Harvey, as he instructed us to do." The other men nodded and went back to their work.

Belle and Grace joined the women from the Guild, who were setting up the tables where the gingerbread houses for the raffle would go on display. A little stage had been constructed in the front for the school kids' nativity play. People were also unloading chairs which they had borrowed from the local church for some of the older folk.

Wilma was there, amid everything, bustling about and organizing. Somehow, she has acquired a megaphone and was using it to good effect to direct people to where they needed to be.

"Grace, Belle. Over here!" she called. "We need some more extension cables for the Christmas lights. Are the gingerbread houses ready to be photographed?"

"I'll see if we can find some more cables," said Gram. "Belle, why don't you show Wilma the photos of the gingerbread houses that you already took? You can ask her where the hot chocolate booth should go."

Belle sighed. "Better get it over with," she muttered. She took a deep breath and walked over to where Wilma stood.

"Hi Wilma," she said brightly. "Great job on the organizing. I was wondering where you wanted me to set up for the Singalong?"

Wilma's face went into a fixed smile. "Belle! So glad you offered your services and your hot chocolate booth! I hear it's going well? It's a pity that Harvey didn't let the Women's Guild run it again this year, but I suppose he thought he needed something trendier and hipper."

Belle could feel the eyes of the women from the Guild on her and she knew that needed to be careful about what she said. "Um, yes Wilma. The hot chocolate is going really well, thanks to all the work you did in advertising last year."

Wilma nodded, her smile getting tighter. "I was worried that people might not want to line up for hot chocolate from someone else, but it seems like they're happy to try something new."

Belle felt annoyance rise in her, but she managed to keep her voice even. "Yes, well, I experimented a little with the recipe."

"Good heavens! Experimental hot chocolate!" boomed Wilma, even without the megaphone. "Now, I don't think we have a whole lot of space for an extra booth, but we could make some space at the back there." She pointed to an awkward spot behind the other booths. "Do you need some help to set up?"

Belle thought she would be lucky if she sold any mugs of hot chocolate at all, if she set up her booth where the woman was pointing, but she didn't want to tell Wilma that. She pasted a smile on her face. "Sure. I'll make sure I'm all set up and ready to go!"

Wilma nodded like a woman who had successfully warded off a challenge. "Good, good. Well, I have to go now, but if you're having any problems, just let me know." And then she was gone, off to yell through her megaphone at some other poor soul.

Belle sighed and went back over to help some of the women stringing fairy lights around the square. Grace was already plugging them into the extension cables that she had found.

"Well done, my dear," said Grace, as she plugged in the last light. "Wilma can be overwhelming."

Belle nodded. "Yes, but I think that I've just agreed to set up my booth in a spot where no one will see it."

"Never mind that. It will all work out on the night, you'll see," said Grace with a twinkle in her eye. "Now, do you want to help me offer the shortbread around, or should I ask Wilma to command someone else?"

Belle laughed. "I'll help you offer the shortbread around, Gram." She took the container of biscuits and walked around to offer all the volunteers something to snack on.

As she approached a group of women, she could overhear their conversation.

"It's going to be a disaster," said one woman, her voice trembling. "No one is going to want to come and sing carols when the tree farmer—who supplied the enormous Christmas tree and all the Christmas lights for the Singalong—is in jail!"

"Nonsense," said another person, briskly putting an arm around the woman's shoulders. "Now that they have found the killer and arrested him, we can all sleep well in our beds."

"I still can't believe it," said the first woman, her voice wobbling. "He was always so jolly and happy. We all know now that he has been a wolf in sheep's clothing all along."

Belle couldn't help herself. Showing them all a shocked face, she interrupted their conversation. "You can't honestly believe that Harvey did this?

The women all looked at her like she was mad.

"We don't know what he is capable of," said one, her voice a little more sympathetic. "He could have done it, you never know."

"Well, I believe him when he says that he didn't kill that woman," said Belle stoutly. "He's innocent and we all know it."

The women glanced at each other, their faces a mix of skepticism. But before any of them could say anything else, Belle had turned away and was offering shortbread to the men working on the large Christmas tree.

By the time Belle had returned to help Gram with a section of fairy lights, she was so angry that she could barely string the lights up straight.

"Why is everyone talking about Harvey like he's the murderer?" asked Belle. "What happened to being innocent until proven guilty?"

Grace sighed and put her arm around Belle's shoulders. "I don't know, honey. People around here should know better. I agree with you. Harvey is a good man and we should all believe in him."

Belle nodded. Harvey had few friends at the moment. "We will just have to help find the actual murderer," she said, with determination.

Chapter 15

It was the twenty-first of December and the evening of the Singalong had finally arrived. The perpetual snow clouds had miraculously cleared just in time, and the stars sparkled brightly.

Belle parked her station wagon on the side of the road at the back of the old market square, behind several other cars.

"Goodness, it looks like we'll have a good turnout," said Grace, gazing at the crowds of people flocking into the old market square. Everyone was bundled up in thick coats and warm scarves. Belle's grandmother sat in the passenger seat, looking about excitedly. "I can't wait to sing some carols!"

"Good thing that I finished work early," said Belle, as a group of school kids wandered past in their costumes for the nativity play. "I hope Jerry has delivered my booth to the right spot. Wilma said there was space for me near the rear entrance, but I can't see it."

Jerry had offered to lift Belle's little wooden booth into one of the large delivery trucks that they used for the Christmas trees and to drop it off in the market square, in time for the Singalong.

The loyal farmhand had done his best to keep Harvey's Christmas Tree farm running. Meanwhile, Harvey waited in the county lockup for a judge to determine whether or not he would be allowed out on bail before Christmas. Even so, there were hardly any customers coming to buy Christmas trees anymore. Jerry had reassured her it was normal for sales to drop off closer to Christmas. But Belle couldn't help but worry that the lack of customers had less to do with the fact that it was almost Christmas and more to do with the fact that Harvey was currently in jail.

"I sure hope that Harvey gets out soon." Belle glanced at Grace, all bundled up in a thick coat and scarf like everyone else. "Jerry can't keep everything running by himself forever."

"He's doing his best." Grace reached over and squeezed Belle's hand. "I'm sure Harvey will be out on bail soon. Christmas is almost here, at least! And then after that, it'll be New Year's Eve. I'm so excited!"

Belle could not help but think that even if Harvey was released on bail, it was only the start of his problems. He would still need to prove his innocence. But she managed to smile at Gram's determined festive cheer, and turned to gaze at the market square.

The town center looked more cheerful than usual. With the enormous Christmas tree and the fairy lights strung around the open space, it was a twinkly winter wonderland. A group of carolers were already singing nearby, and the smell of roasted chestnuts floated through the air.

Belle got out of the car and then helped Gram out of her side. They both pulled their coats tighter around themselves in the chill winter air. Gram switched on her little flashlight so that they could see where they were going.

"Hey! Didn't Wilma ban flashlights in case they detract from the Christmas lights?" asked Belle, chuckling.

"Who cares what Wilma says," replied Grace, waving her flashlight about rebelliously. "This is a special night! We're going to have so much fun! And to do that, we need to see where we're going."

Just then, Belle spotted Jerry walking towards them from across the square.

"There you are!" she called out, as he got closer. "Thanks for doing this, Jerry. You know, keeping Harvey's business running, putting up the Christmas tree for the Singalong, and then even moving my booth for me."

"No problem, Belle." Jerry grinned at her. "Harvey would do the same for me if the tables were turned."

"I hope he'll be released soon. Did you get your lawyer friend to help?"

Jerry nodded. "He's putting up bail tomorrow morning."

"That's great news!" Belle felt a tremendous wave of relief. She hadn't wanted to tell her grandmother, but she had been really worried that Harvey might not be released on bail at all.

Jerry shook his head. "The case is still looking pretty bad for him though. I'm sure you know that, Belle."

"Do I?" asked Belle with a frown. "I mean, of course it's bad. But how can anyone prove Harvey did something he didn't do?"

Jerry shrugged. "I'm no lawyer, Belle. But you've got to admit that Harvey has made some mistakes having an affair with a married lady. Lending money to her and everything. And then her body being found on his farm on the very day she was supposed to repay the loan. Things don't look good."

Belle bit her lip as she thought of poor Harvey all alone in a cell, probably feeling hopeless. She would have visited him, but the judge had said that no visitors were allowed until the bail hearing.

"Do you think Harvey could have killed Victoria Dunn?"

Jerry shook his head quickly. "No way! But, unfortunately for him, it's the judge who will have to be convinced of that."

"We need to find out more about Victoria and what she was doing at the tree farm that evening," Belle said with decision.

"First things first," said Grace, who had been listening to their hushed conversation. "We need to get your booth up and running, otherwise we will miss the Singalong altogether. What time is it?"

Jerry checked his watch. "It's almost five-thirty. The Singalong starts in an hour."

Belle looked around for her little wooden booth. "Um, I can't see where my booth is."

Wilma had distinctly said that there was only room for her at the back entrance.

"I delivered it where your grandmother told me to set it down. It's right over there," said Jerry. He pointed to the front entrance. "You can't miss it."

Belle followed his pointing finger. There, in the front entrance of the old market square, in prime position next to the pancake stand, was her little wooden booth. Someone had decorated it with sprigs of holly and a large Christmas bow, ready for her to set up her Crock-Pot.

"That's quite a long way from where I expected to set up," she said, glancing over at her grandmother, her eyebrows raised. "Thanks, Jerry."

Grace's face had taken on a determined look.

"No problem, Belle." Jerry winked at her, then walked away.

"Gram? You know that Wilma is going to be furious, right?" said Belle, as they made their way to her little booth.

"I know," said Grace, nodding her head. "But I won't let her push us around. This is our Singalong too." She puffed out her chest. "And I did not spend the last week constructing the best gingerbread houses in the county to be taking instructions from her."

Belle chuckled at her grandmother's stubbornness. It was one of the things she loved most about her.

When they had arranged the decorations on the booth, Belle quickly fetched the packets of cocoa, sugar, and marshmallows from the station wagon, as well as her spices of nutmeg, allspice, cloves, and cinnamon. She set them out on the little wooden table next to the Crock-Pot. Only when she had all of her ingredients set out and ready, did Belle start making her special hot chocolate, with Grace's help.

By this time, more people had arrived and there was a little line forming in front of the pancake stand next door. Someone was handing out apple cider in paper cups and children were running around excitedly. The roasting chestnuts were drawing a lot of attention and soon the aroma of cinnamon and spices permeated the square. Across the way, Belle saw Doris selling raffle tickets for the gingerbread houses on display.

Her first customers were a group of three women who looked about interestedly. They ordered a cup of hot chocolate each.

Belle handed the first lady a cup, and she took a sip, her eyes widening at the taste.

"Oh, my!" she said, her face lighting up with surprise. "This is superb! What's your recipe?"

Belle handed the other two ladies a cup each. "It's a secret," she replied with a smile.

The women were looking around. "This is a much bigger event than back in Hollydale," one of them said. "We had hoped our fireworks would have attracted a crowd but it seems everyone came here instead."

Belle couldn't help but interrupt. "You're from Hollydale?" she asked.

"Yes, we're from the Hollydale Women's Craft Club," said one of them, shrugging a shoulder. "We're here to check out the Cherryville Singalong and report back to the others." She winked. "Rumor has it that Wilma is planning to use some kind of fancy technology and we want to find out what it is. You know, in case we need to up our game next year."

"Hollydale, you say?" said Grace, loudly. "Well, my granddaughter here would like to ask you some questions."

Belle suddenly found herself being observed by at least four pairs of eyes.

Chapter 16

"She wants to ask you if any of you knew Victoria Dunn," said Grace loudly to the women from the neighboring town, before Belle could stop her. "We heard that she was also from Hollydale."

"Yes, she was," said one lady in a hushed tone. "It's terrible what happened to her. She went missing less than a week ago. And then we heard the news. Very shocking."

"Victoria used to sing a solo at our Singalongs," another woman said sadly. "She was fantastic."

Goose bumps rose on Belle's arms. This was the first time that she had encountered someone who knew the unfortunate Victoria Dunn. "Do you know if Victoria had any enemies? Anyone who would want to hurt her?" she asked.

"Oh, my goodness, I don't think so," said the first lady who had ordered a cup of hot chocolate. "She was such a lovely-looking woman, and she sang like an angel. But she and her husband had only recently moved to our town, so we hadn't known her long. Her poor husband is most distraught."

"I heard that she had some money problems," said another Hollydale resident. "I heard her quarrelling with her husband about it once. She was quite horrible to him."

Belle's ears pricked up at this new information.

"Do you know what sort of money problems?" She wondered if these women knew that Victoria had been in debt, or that she had borrowed money from Harvey.

"I'm not sure. But you know how these things can escalate." The woman waved her hand dismissively.

"And now poor Mr. Dunn is selling their beautiful house and leaving town. I don't blame him. There are too many memories for him there, I guess. But his house won't be on the market long. People are viewing it every day. I heard that he's had several offers already."

"What about friends and family? Do you think that they might know more?" asked Belle.

The first Hollydale woman, put her head to the side as she considered the question. "Don't think she had any friends and family," she sipped her hot chocolate cup delicately. "Anyway, we have to go. We won't get a good spot if we don't hurry up."

"Okay, I hope you enjoy the Singalong." Belle inclined her head politely.

The ladies took their cups and strolled away into the crowd, talking in low voices amongst themselves.

A moment later, Wilma arrived, driving her minivan. When she saw Belle and her Crock-Pot at the front entrance, her eyebrows drew together. She parked right in front of Belle's booth and hopped out.

"What are you doing here?" she demanded. "You're supposed to be at the back."

"Jerry must have gotten the wrong message and brought it here," said Grace, shrugging. "Oh well, I guess that it's too late to move it now, so we will just have to stay where we are."

Wilma pursed her lips like she had swallowed something sour. "I guess so. I have to fetch the cables." She stomped off without another word.

Belle raised her eyebrows at her grandmother as if to say "I told you so."

Grace just shrugged and poked out her tongue.

A few moments later, Wilma returned with a large crate of cables from the back of her minivan.

"What are those?" Belle asked, trying to change the topic. She looked inside the crate.

"I borrowed them from the school," Wilma said shortly. "Everyone is arriving and I still need to get the big screen TV ready."

"What big screen TV?" asked Grace, perplexed. "I thought you were just borrowing a small screen."

Wilma pointed to a massive new structure that had been set up next to the Christmas tree. It was a large dark metal frame, with a giant rectangle attached to the top of it.

"The screen is for showing the words of the carols clear to the back of the crowd," Wilma explained. "I rented it. I figured with all this new technology that we could really impress everyone."

Grace's eyes widened. "My goodness, how did you get that in here?" she asked.

"Oh, it was pretty easy," said Wilma. "I just had to drive slowly, so the screen wouldn't fall off my trailer."

"It needed a *trailer*?" asked Grace, shocked. "How big is it?"

"Bigger than anything that Hollydale has arranged for their pathetic Singalong, I can tell you that," said Wilma smugly. "And there are speakers too."

She lifted the crate of cables and headed toward the Christmas tree that was already blazing with light. Fairy lights glowed along the edge of the buildings around the old market square and the trees lining the street were strung with lights, too.

"I'm not sure that's such a good idea," said Belle to Wilma's back, as they followed her to the square. "It looks like an awful lot of electricity is going to be needed for the lights and now the big screen TV. We might blow a fuse."

Wilma snorted. "Don't worry, I have it all figured out," she said.

Belle and Grace gave each other a meaningful look as Wilma fussed off to where the big screen towered over the Christmas tree. They could see her busily plugging in the cables and turning on the laptop that was used to project the words onto the screen. The sign beside her read: "Carols and Christmas Lights – Sponsored by the Cherryville Women's Guild."

From her vantage point at the front entrance, Belle could see that there were a great many cables and that they were all tangled in a mess. She watched Doris trying to untangle them, without a flashlight.

"I think I'll just go and help Doris," said Grace, spotting her friend struggling. She trotted off toward the knotty cables, bringing her industrial-strength flashlight to the rescue, while Belle returned to her booth.

By this time, the market square had become quite crowded and Belle spent the next twenty minutes selling cup after cup of her spiced hot chocolate topped with marshmallows.

A squawk from the speakers announced the start of the concert. Everyone waited with bated breath. Then the big screen came alive, and the sound of "Jingle Bells" blared around the square. The small crowd that had already gathered started clapping.

Wilma beamed with pride and fiddled with the computer so that the words of the carols showed up on the screen and began scrolling past. Everyone cheered and clapped.

Belle chuckled in surprise. "Well, maybe Wilma has done it after all," she said to herself, as she watched the President of the Cherryville Women's Guild take center stage.

Wilma looked very pleased with herself. She raised a microphone to her mouth. "Good evening, everyone." Her voice boomed over the loudspeaker. "Welcome to our first ever high-tech Singalong!"

The speakers roared to life with bass music and the small crowd cheered and started singing "Jingle Bells" again, louder this time. The lights all around the market square blazed brightly, with those on the Christmas Tree glowing the brightest of all. Words of the carols flashed across the screen.

"Great idea of Wilma's," commented a man standing near Belle's booth. "Clever of the Women's Guild to get that big screen TV up and running."

Belle could see the faces of the sour women from Hollydale. They looked like a defeated football team.

Suddenly, the big screen TV flickered and then went blank. And so did every light in the square.

Everything plunged into darkness.

"What happened?" Wilma's voice called out from the stage, panic in her voice. "Did a plug fall out?"

Grace flicked on her flashlight and aimed it toward the knot of tangled cables. Doris joined her and together they tried to untangle the cables.

"I can't see a thing," Grace called out to Wilma above the crowd's chatter. "I think we have a lot more problems than a blown fuse. I have no idea which one needs fixing."

The ladies from Hollydale were now grinning and whispering to each other.

A few women from the Woman's Guild went to help Grace and Doris, their prohibited flashlights bobbing in the dark.

Several minutes later, the stage was still dark as many of the townsfolk turned to leave.

"There will be a little delay, folks," called Wilma from the stage, her voice wobbling a little. "If you will just be patient."

Some of the remaining crowd muttered and Belle saw quite a few people looking angry and disappointed. A kid started crying.

"Oh no, I was so looking forward to the Singalong," said someone behind Belle. "What a shame."

A few people used their phones as flashlights to see where they were going.

"This is so embarrassing." Grace chuckled. "Wilma will never live this down!"

"Wait, why don't we just sing the carols the old-fashioned way?" Jerry's voice called out in the darkness. "Anyone got any candles?"

"I brought some just in case," called out one of the women from Hollydale. "You know, because of the whole flashlight ban." She dug in her bag and handed them out.

A cheer went up in the crowd and someone started singing "We Wish You a Merry Christmas." Soon enough, everyone joined in and the square filled with the sound of people singing. Someone had brought a guitar and strummed along with the singing.

Belle couldn't help but laugh. The big screen had not worked, but at least there was still quite a crowd in the old market square and people seemed to be having a good time.

But even as she mouthed the words to the Christmas carols, she couldn't help but think about what the Hollydale ladies had told her earlier that evening.

Poor Victoria Dunn hardly had any family or friends and now her heartbroken husband was leaving town. Belle thought about Mr. Dunn selling their house. Would it be enough to pay off Victoria's debts? She remembered Sheriff Barnes saying that he had spoken to Mr. Dunn.

So, the police knew about Victoria Dunn's debts. But they had arrested Harvey anyway!

A thoughtful expression came over Belle's face. If Mr. Dunn was selling his house and was showing it to the public, it seemed like an excellent opportunity to ask him if he knew of anyone else who may have loaned his wife money. Anyone who may have been ready to kill the poor woman for money.

Maybe I can slip into a house viewing and ask him a few questions.

Chapter 17

"I think you need to fill it up with gas," said Grace, leaning in through the car window and eyeing the gauge nervously.

Mittens wandered around sniffing at the car tires, his little feet making cat paw prints in the snow.

"It's fine. I filled it up yesterday. I have to get going." Belle opened the car door and swung into the driver's seat.

"Maybe I haven't packed enough food for you." Grace glanced at the little basket on the passenger seat with sandwiches, an apple, several baked goods, and a small thermos of coffee. "Let me get some more from the kitchen. I have a fresh batch of drop biscuits coming out of the oven in a few minutes."

"No, I'll be fine," Belle said, patting Grace's arm. "I have more than enough to eat. Besides, I won't be gone for more than a few hours. It's not like I'm going to an island with no food on it or something."

"But you're driving all the way to Hollydale, my dear."

Belle rolled her eyes. "It's only an hour's drive, Gram. It's not far."

Mittens nudged Grace's leg. She picked him up and held him close.

"You be good, Mittens," said Belle. "I'll be back before you know it."

Her grandmother looked concerned. "I still think you should leave this to Sheriff Barnes. He's the one who should be investigating Victoria's death."

Belle shook her head. "He thinks he's solved the case by arresting poor Harvey. I can't sit here and do nothing." She gave her grandmother an imploring look. "Plus, I'll just be going to a house viewing. Loads of people are looking at the house every day, apparently. I have to at least try to see if he knows anything helpful before he sells his house and leaves. Victoria's husband may be the only one who knows who she borrowed money from and if there's anyone who may have wanted to harm her." She pulled her seatbelt across her torso and fastened it with decision. "If I can find out what he knows about Victoria's debts, then maybe we can get the sheriff to release Harvey and investigate the case some more."

"All right, but be careful," Grace said, still unsure. "Make sure that there are other people around. And if you get into trouble, you call me immediately."

Belle nodded. She put the car in reverse and backed out of the driveway, waving goodbye to her grandmother from the window. "Behave yourself, Mittens! I won't be gone for long. Watch out for mice."

She put the car in gear and headed down the street. It was a beautiful day. The sun was shining and the snow was glittering. All of the bright Christmas decorations in the yards of the houses added to the festive atmosphere.

But as much as Belle loved seeing the decorations and the feeling of her favorite time of year, her heart was heavy. She could not help but worry about Harvey and what might happen to him if she didn't find out who was responsible for Victoria's death.

She cruised along the highway; her stomach fluttering with nervous energy as she drove closer and closer to the neighboring town. It wouldn't be hard to find out where Victoria lived. In her experience of small towns, all Belle had to do was visit the general store on the main drag and ask the people at the cash registers any questions. If their staff was anything like Mrs. Haggerty, she could find out not only where Victoria Dunn lived, but also what the entire town thought of her and about the recent events.

Small town gossip could often reveal more information than an FBI investigation.

Belle rolled down the window and let the fresh air flow over her, pushing back her chestnut hair that had escaped from her ponytail. She glanced at the clock on the dash, it read nine o'clock. She calculated that the drive would take her just over an hour.

She turned on the radio and listened to some country music as she settled in for a long drive.

By the time she reached Hollydale, it was already busy with Christmas shoppers. It didn't take Belle long to find the general store. A large sign was attached to the front of the building that read 'Bill's General Store', with an image of a red wagon filled with boxes of merchandise.

Belle parked her car on the street, got out, and stretched. She paused on the sidewalk. It looked like a regular general store—nothing too fancy. As she headed inside, she thought it was busy for a small-town grocery store. There were several people in line at the cash register, all chatting away. Belle made her way to the front of the line, feeling a little out of place.

The cashier, a plump woman in her forties with curly red hair and wire-rimmed glasses, looked up as Belle approached. "Hi there," she said warmly. "What can I help you find today?"

Belle swallowed. "I was wondering if you could tell me where the Dunns live. Lived," she said, correcting herself at the last minute. "Where Victoria Dunn lived with... her husband. I heard that their house was on the market." It occurred to Belle that she didn't know what to call Mr. Dunn other than... Mr. Dunn.

The cashier's smile faded slightly. "Victoria Dunn, you say?" she asked. "I hate to tell you, but there was an unfortunate incident last week. Victoria was killed over in another town." She leaned forward conspiratorially, in a manner not unlike Mrs. Haggerty. "They think she was murdered. By the guy that she was having an affair with. He runs some kind of farm."

Several of the women standing in the line nodded and tut-tutted their disapproval.

"Yes, I heard something about that," Belle said. "Did you know Victoria Dunn?"

The cashier narrowed her eyes at Belle suspiciously. "Why do you want to know?"

Belle said the first thing that came into her head. "Oh, no reason. I just heard that Mr. Dunn was selling their wonderful house. Thought I may take a look..." She hoped she looked like someone who could afford to buy a big house and not like a nosy neighbor who just wanted view a dead woman's home. "I'm from Cherryville," she added.

The cashier looked shocked. "You're from the town with the guy that they arrested for killing her? Better be careful living in a place like that!"

Belle was glad that Wilma Figg wasn't around to hear that.

"Yes, well, perhaps I should buy some flowers to take with me. Do you know where I can buy some?"

The cashier's wariness faded, and she nodded. "We don't have a florist in town. But we have some fresh cut daisies and sunflowers in the store. And I can tell you how to get to the Dunn's house. Just take a right at the end of the street and it'll be the first house on the left. You can't miss it. There are big billboards and house viewings for purchasers every day. It's the most expensive house in the area."

Belle grabbed a bunch of flowers and stood in the line to pay for them, but all the ladies waved her forward. They were content to stand around and chat. Perhaps that was why the store was busy. It was where everyone came to hear the latest news.

"I didn't know Victoria Dunn well, but nobody deserves to be murdered," one woman said.

Belle listened to them gossiping about Victoria Dunn with interest, trying hard not to look like she was there to find out information. She handed over some notes for the flowers and the cashier opened the register.

"That's true," another woman added. "And when they find that boyfriend of hers, he'll be in a world of trouble too."

Belle thought of Harvey currently in the county lockup and figured that he was already in a world of trouble.

"Yes, we all saw Victoria going for lunch at the Spicy Olive with that guy, didn't we, ladies?" The woman looked around the group, who all nodded.

The cashier gave Belle a knowing look as she handed her some coins in change together with a receipt. "She had lunch there with that guy who looked like he could have been a lumberjack," she said. "And they even stayed all night at the hotel, can you believe it? My cousin works there is a cleaner and she told me. We all wondered what Victoria Dunn was doing with him, in her fancy clothes and all. But then we heard he had his own business, and it all made sense."

Belle raised her eyebrows. "How did it make sense?"

The cashier shrugged. "Everyone knew how much debt she was in. She owed money to most of the shops in this town, but that didn't stop her from spending. Victoria would come into town and drop hundreds of dollars on luxury items like chocolates and designer handbags." She made a face. "So, when we saw her cozying up to some guy with his own business, we all thought that it would be to get money out of him."

Her jaw dropped. The gossip in this town was worse than back home. But then they were probably right.

"I feel so sorry for Mr. Dunn though; so embarrassing for him," said a woman wearing a knitted purple scarf. "He's such a nice man. And so handsome too."

The cashier nodded. "Poor Mr. Dunn. Everyone talking about him and all. And now he has to sell his house to pay for all of Victoria's debts." She pointed to the communal noticeboard where many flyers were pinned up.

Belle walked over to have a look. Sure enough, the biggest flyer had pictures of a house for sale. And there, in black and white, was the address for the place. She took out her phone and snapped a picture of the flyer.

"Thanks for your help," she said, turning to leave.

"Sure. Have a good day," replied the cashier with a nod. "Like I said, just take a right at the end of the street and it'll be the first house on the left. You can take pictures to show everyone when you get back home." She winked at Belle, knowingly.

Belle straightened her back and tried to look like she had not just traveled over an hour to listen to gossip. Holding the little posy of flowers, she walked out into the cold winter air.

Chapter 18

Belle pulled up in front of the for-sale sign and gazed at the building behind it. She wasn't sure what she had expected Victoria Dunn's house to look like, but she was sure this wasn't it. It looked more like a hotel than someone's home.

It was two stories tall and had a grand entrance with large white columns flanking the door. Belle could even see a balcony on the second story. Expensive Christmas lights adorned the roof and porch, and the garden looked like it had been professionally laid out and manicured.

The Dunn's mansion couldn't be more different than Grace's homely cottage. Belle thought of her grandmother's comfortable living room with its worn couch and threadbare throw rugs. The Christmas tree that came out every year was strung with the same handmade decorations. Their little home was filled with Grace's knickknacks and the walls were covered in pictures of Belle growing up. There were also plenty of photographs of Mittens doing silly things and playing with his cat toys.

Belle's breath fogged up the car window. The heater had made the inside of the station wagon nice and warm again during the short drive from the grocery store, and Belle was loath to step back out into the cold. She glanced at the little clutch of cheerful daisies on the passenger seat. "Perhaps I should have bought a bigger bunch of flowers," she muttered.

But then the thought of Harvey popped into her head. The sad look on his face as he sat in the back of Sheriff Barnes' police car. She couldn't let him spend Christmas in the county lockup. He had done so much for her, helping her set up the hot chocolate booth when she needed a job. She had to help him when he needed it.

Belle pulled her woolen hat over her ears, tidied her scarf, and drew a deep breath. Then she opened the door and got out of the car, making her way past the for-sale sign, up to the pristine paved path that led to the front door. The for-sale sign had "daily viewings" emblazoned across it. But, looking around, Belle couldn't see anyone else.

I guess everybody must be inside, viewing the house.

It was pretty cold outside after all. No one would want to stand outside for long.

Belle walked up to the entrance and pressed the buzzer. A few moments later, a man in a suit opened the door. He looked surprised to see her.

"There are no house viewings today," he said gruffly. "Short notice cancellation of all of that, I'm afraid."

Belle's heart sank. "Oh dear, I'm sorry to bother you," she said politely, wondering if this fellow was a real estate agent. He was handsome, with a flashy salesman look about him. "I just hoped to view the house today. I heard it was on the market. My name is Belle; I'm from the next town over. You know, Cherryville. It's a bit of a drive."

"And you want to see the house now in case you may like to buy it?" The man looked at the flowers in her hand. "Well, if you want to have a look now, then I guess I can make time." He stepped back from the doorway to let her in.

Belle entered the house hesitantly. She looked around the grand entrance hall with its high ceiling and marble floor. "This is delightful," she said, trying to sound interested, and hoping that she looked richer than she was.

"Yes, it is. My wife and I bought it a few years ago. She loved it here." There was a sadness in his voice.

"Oh! You're Mr. Dunn. I'm so sorry; I just assumed that you were the real estate agent. I'm sorry to hear that your wife passed away." She held out the flowers. "These are for you."

"Thank you. Yes, it was very sudden. She died a few weeks ago." He took the flowers, then paused for a moment, lost in thought. "Anyway, shall we look around the house?"

He showed her around the hallway, pointing out the features that his wife had loved. Belle tried to act interested yet respectful. Then he led her into a large, open-plan living room with modern furniture. It looked like something out of a decor magazine. Elegant white curtains were pulled to the side with tasseled cords and the spotless windows looked like they had been freshly cleaned by an army of servants.

Strangely enough, there were no Christmas decorations inside, anywhere. After all the festive cheer, the lack of Christmas decorations made the whole place feel bereft.

"This was her favorite room," he said, gesturing around the room. "She loved to entertain guests here."

"I'm sure it must be very difficult for you. Especially at this time of year." She wondered how she could possibly ask this well-dressed man about his wife's debts.

Suddenly, the whole idea of her trip seemed a bit silly and Belle wondered what on earth she could have been thinking? She had expected lots of people to be around, not a private tour.

"Yes, it is," he replied, shortly. "Belle did you say? I think the police said that a person called Belle discovered my wife and called them?"

"Um, yes, that's me. I just found her, that's all," Belle said quickly. "I was working at the Christmas Tree Farm, the hot chocolate booth actually, and was passing by the... ah area, when I saw your wife's coat." Belle hesitated to say the word *dumpster*. It didn't seem right to mention that here. "And soon after that, Sheriff Barnes arrived and took over."

He nodded slowly, thoughtfully.

"That was nice of you to come all the way out here. I hope that you like the house. Please, have a seat. We can go upstairs in a minute," he said, gesturing to an elegant white couch.

Belle sat down, feeling very out of place.

"I hope you don't mind," Dunn said, as he stood holding the bunch of daisies, "but I just need to make an important call." He gestured toward the other room, where Belle assumed an office was located.

He turned and walked into the other room, closing the door behind him. Belle sat on the white couch, waiting for him to return. Suddenly, she felt extremely awkward. There was no way that he would talk about his dead wife's debts in front of a stranger like herself. Especially since she had said that her reason for visiting was to view the house.

Remembering her grandmother's instructions, it occurred to Belle that perhaps she should let Sheriff Barnes know where she was. Better to be safe than sorry. She pulled her phone out of her bag and quickly tapped out a text to Sheriff Barnes.

While she waited for a response, Belle looked around the room. There was a large abstract painting on the wall opposite her. It was mostly shades of blue and green, with splashes of bright yellow and orange.

Not all that pretty, but probably very expensive.

She couldn't help but wonder how much money Victoria's husband made. He surely must be well-off to afford such an expensive-looking house, paintings and all. She had no idea what he did for a living. In fact, come to think about it, she knew nothing about him at all.

As if on cue, Mr. Dunn suddenly entered the room again. "I'm sorry," he said, "I don't know your surname. I'm sure you've already mentioned it."

"Beaumont," she replied, taking her courage in both of her hands. "Belle Beaumont. I was wondering if perhaps you knew who may have wanted to harm your wife? Do you think it could have been somebody she owed money to?"

Dunn's face darkened and he scowled. "I don't know," he said, after a long moment of silence. "I've already been questioned by the sheriff about that. As far as I know, Victoria didn't have any enemies. She certainly never mentioned anything to me. But then my wife kept a lot of secrets."

Belle clamped her lips together and nodded in what she hoped was a sympathetic way.

"But you're not here about the house, are you? You're here for the gossip." He smiled suddenly, in a way that didn't reach his eyes.

A tingle at the back of her neck made the hair there feel like it stood on end. She hesitated, wondering if it wasn't time to leave after all.

"Oh, no, not at all," she hastened to reassure him. "I'm so sorry. I didn't mean to pry."

Mr. Dunn shrugged. "It doesn't matter now, does it?" he said coolly. "Everyone knows that Victoria wanted a divorce. I think that she only married me for my money."

Belle was taken aback. "Did she tell you that?"

He nodded, his face hardening. "She came to me one day, about a month ago, and told me that she wanted a divorce. She was tired of me and she wanted to be with some guy in a plaid shirt instead. I tried to convince her that we could work it out, but she wouldn't hear anything of it."

He paused, staring into the distance.

By now, Belle was feeling very uncomfortable, and not just from sitting on the fashionable yet narrow couch. Victoria's husband seemed to be a very different person to the grieving fellow that she had imagined. He was a handsome man, but in a cold and austere way.

"I followed her a few times, you know, watching as she made me the laughingstock of the whole county. I saw her with him on more than one occasion. They liked to go to my favorite restaurant, the Spicy Olive. And then stay there at the hotel. Have you been there?"

The man was strangely calm for someone who obviously thought he was being mocked by his neighbors. Belle shook her head.

"Anyway, I decided that I had had enough. If she wanted to leave me, then she could go. But I wouldn't let her take half of my money with her. So, I cut up all of her credit cards." He looked up at Belle then, his eyes cold and hard.

"Oh," said Belle awkwardly.

That would explain why a woman who enjoyed shopping as much as Victoria clearly had, had suddenly run up a lot of debts with local traders. It would also explain why she had suddenly needed a lot of money from Harvey to pay her debts.

Belle was beginning to feel a little nauseous. Was it possible that this good-looking, wealthy man had killed his own wife? After all, he had a motive if he really thought of himself as the victim in this whole sordid mess.

"I can see what you're thinking," he interrupted her thoughts. "And I'm wondering whether you're here because you perhaps saw something. Something that you might not tell anyone if I paid you a large sum of money. Isn't that how this kind of encounter usually works?"

Belle looked at him blankly. Was he talking about blackmail? The thought made her skin crawl.

"No," she said firmly, standing up. "I'm sorry. I think you have misunderstood."

Dunn's face changed, and he stood up quickly, towering over her.

Belle was suddenly very aware of how small she was. And what a mistake she had made in coming to Hollydale.

Chapter 19

Mr. Dunn walked over to the curtains and, pulling the tasseled cord from them, drew the expensive fabric across the windows as if to shut out prying eyes. He held the cord in his hand as he turned to face her, contemplating it.

"You know, Belle," he said conversationally, "I never liked the decor in this room. But Victoria insisted on changing everything to look like something that she had seen in a magazine."

Belle's heart skipped a beat. He seemed calmer than before, if that was possible. It seemed like he had been contemplating a problem and had now reached a decision. She looked at the curtain cord in his hand with trepidation, remembering suddenly that Victoria's official cause of death had been strangulation.

Belle's thoughts flickered to the text that she had sent Sheriff Barnes and she hoped against hope that he had read it. In the meantime, she had to keep Mr. Dunn talking. The man seemed to like the sound of his own voice. Perhaps, she could use that to keep him busy.

"I suppose that it's not so bad when you get used to it," Belle said, as steadily as she could. "And now that you're selling the house, I'm sure that the purchaser will really like it." She looked about for an exit. "Have you thought about putting up a Christmas tree?"

"That's true," Mr. Dunn said, nodding. "I'm sure that they will. In fact, I have already accepted an offer for the house for quite a bit of money."

Belle swallowed. "Oh, that's wonderful!" she said, making her voice sound as enthusiastic as possible.

"Yes, that's why the tours of the house have been cancelled. But when you mentioned that your name was Belle, and that you were from Cherryville, I was interested to find out more." He inclined his head in what seemed the direction of the other town. "I have been following everything that the police have discovered about the case, you see. And I remembered that someone called Belle found my wife. In fact, I checked my notes about it in the other room a few minutes ago."

His notes? He has written my name down in his notes?

Just then, Belle's phone rang in her bag. She dug it out quickly as Mr. Dunn lunged and knocked it out of her hand. The phone clattered to the floor and skidded across the pristine oak floorboards.

"No phone calls," Mr. Dunn said, his voice tight.

Belle's heart pounded so hard that she thought it might burst out of her chest. She tried to think of a way out of the situation, but couldn't. The only thing that she could do was stall for time.

"It's probably just my grandmother," Belle said, trying to keep her voice from shaking. "She's probably wondering where I am."

"I don't care who it is," Mr. Dunn said.

Belle swallowed hard and tried to think of a way to get out of the room. She felt the anger emanating from Mr. Dunn in waves and she knew that she didn't have much time.

"Now," said Mr. Dunn, seating himself comfortably once more and crossing his legs. "What exactly did you see last week, Belle Beaumont from Cherryville? I'm sure that you aren't really interested in buying my house."

"Nothing, nothing at all," Belle said earnestly. "I found Victoria in the dumpster behind Harvey's office. And then I called Harvey over. And then we called the police." This time, she didn't hesitate to say the word *dumpster*.

Mr. Dunn narrowed his eyes. "I think you're lying to me, Belle Beaumont. I think you know what really happened."

She looked around the room surreptitiously, but there were only two doors, one of which was closed and presumably lead to the rest of the house. The other was open and led into the hallway and the front door. Belle tried to calculate how quickly she could run to the front door before Mr. Dunn caught up with her. Perhaps the large glass coffee table that stood between them would slow him down somewhat. She knew from experience that walking into a coffee table in the wrong place, and at just the wrong height, could be rather painful.

"I have an idea about what happened," Belle said quietly, eyeing the cord in Mr. Dunn's hand. "I think that you followed Victoria to Harvey's Christmas Tree Farm and waited until no one was looking, then took a strand of tinsel from my hot chocolate booth. Then, you strangled her with it. You're clearly strong enough to lift her into the dumpster, and that's exactly what you did. I don't remember you coming through the car lot, past my hot chocolate booth. So, you must have parked somewhere else along the road so that you could make a quick getaway without anyone seeing you."

Mr. Dunn stood silently near the armchair across from her, as Belle tried to appear as relaxed as possible. She watched as he took a deep breath and then let it out again slowly, before saying conversationally, "You're right."

"I am?" said Belle, surprised.

"I waited until she had finished arguing with that tree farm fellow. I had followed her expensive SUV there, that car I am still paying off. I knew that she was going to tell that fool that she didn't have the money to pay him back. It's what she always did. Spend money and then make me pay off her debts. I thought that it would be the perfect opportunity to kill two birds with one stone, so to speak."

Belle nodded as it all became clear. She remembered the SUV in the parking lot, left there day after day, gathering snow. It must have been Victoria's car all along!

"You killed your wife so that Harvey could take the blame."

"That's right," said Mr. Dunn. "And so far, my plan is working. Except that I didn't factor in...you. Another nosy woman watching me from the sidelines. I'm not sure what you saw that day, but it doesn't matter because you know too much now."

Belle watched as he got up from the armchair and walked toward her. She tried not to panic and clutched the armrest of the sofa tighter.

"Wait, I have a suggestion," she said desperately. "Why don't you let me go right now? I promise not to tell anyone what you told me."

"That's sweet of you, Belle, but sorry, that's simply not an option." He looked at her like she was stupid for even suggesting it.

Just then, there was a loud pounding on the door.

Belle pushed the coffee table sideways. Then she spun on her heel and sprinted to the door.

She heard Mr. Dunn cursing as he banged his shins on the coffee table and tripped up. He recovered quickly, and the sound of his expensive business shoes clacked against the gleaming floorboards behind her.

Belle reached the hallway and had her hand on the door handle, but she wasn't fast enough. Mr. Dunn grabbed hold of her arm and dragged her toward the living room, toward him. Belle struggled desperately against his grip, but he was too strong for her. She knew that time was running out.

"Open up, this is the police!" came the booming voice of Sheriff Barnes from the other side of the door.

Mr. Dunn gasped. "You called the police? How?"

Taking advantage of his momentary surprise, Belle spun against his grip, evaded his clutches and made it to the door. She fumbled with the lock, her fingers trembling, and twisted the handle, yanking the door open.

"Hands in the air!" she heard Sheriff Barnes shout. "You're under arrest for the murder of Victoria Dunn."

Belle looked behind her as Mr. Dunn's hands went up in the air. The sheriff strode into the room with two uniformed policemen following him closely. Belle's knees buckled with relief as she sat down on the floor, closing her eyes.

After a moment, she heard Sheriff Barnes' voice in front of her saying, "Are you okay?"

She opened her eyes and saw him crouched beside her, looking concerned. She nodded quickly, trying hard not to cry. He put his hand on her shoulder and gave it a light squeeze before standing up and reading Mr. Dunn his rights.

Belle watched as he was led from the room by the two Hollydale police officers, his face a picture of shock and disbelief. She couldn't help but feel a great sense of satisfaction at seeing him being led away in handcuffs.

"How did you know that I was in trouble?" she asked Sheriff Barnes.

"Well, you answered my phone call earlier, then I heard your phone fall on the floor or something, but I could still hear your conversation," he said with a grin. He pulled a face. "And of course, there was your grandmother. She took the bus into town and invaded my office at the station. She demanded that I make myself useful and follow you to Hollydale. When you phoned, we recorded it all, and we were able to pinpoint your location. Goodness knows what would have happened if we hadn't turned up when we did. Good job answering your phone like that."

Belle remembered her phone being knocked out of her hand. It was probably still lying on the floor in the other room. She must have answered the call without knowing it. It had been the sheriff calling.

"To be honest with you, I had a feeling that things might not be as they seemed when I talked to Mr. Dunn earlier today," continued the sheriff. "He was trying way too hard to convince me that he was as much a victim as his wife was."

Belle shivered. "It was all so calculated. He planned everything from the beginning."

Sheriff Barnes nodded. "Yes, it certainly looks that way. We'll need to question him further, but I think that he might have given us the answers that we've been looking for, while he was speaking to you." He gave her a quizzical look. "Your grandmother can be quite bossy you know. There was no stopping her from telling me what to do at the police station earlier this morning!"

"That sounds like her." Belle laughed. She was relieved that Sheriff Barnes had saved her in the nick of time.

"I guess this means that we have cleared Harvey's name then?" she asked.

The sheriff grinned. "Yes, I think we can safely say that Harvey is no longer a suspect."

Belle's heart lit up with relief and happiness. She couldn't wait to tell Harvey the good news. It was beginning to look like Christmas might be saved after all.

Chapter 20

"And we need the cranberry sauce, dear," said Grace as she bustled about in the warm kitchen. "Can you get that for me? It's in that pot." She pointed at one of the many pots on the stovetop.

Mittens, highly interested in anything that happened in the kitchen, kept getting underfoot. Belle shooed him out of the way. By way of distraction, she gave him a chew-treat which he seized upon gleefully, taking it to his pet bed in the corner of the kitchen.

"Do you think that we have enough food?" asked Belle, half-jokingly. She had to raise her voice to be heard over the jolly carols that blared from the little radio on the kitchen counter.

It was Christmas Day. The kitchen table was laden with Christmas lunch—and not just any Christmas lunch—Gram's special Christmas roast turkey lunch. There were crispy roast potatoes, tender steamed green beans, buttered carrots with cracked pepper, herb stuffing, and a delicious rich gravy made from a special family recipe. Also, minted peas, mashed potatoes, and those little mini-sausages that Grace liked to cook in the oven over the turkey while it roasted. In the tiny spaces between the plates and bowls of steaming food, there were Christmas crackers, paper party hats, and plates of mince pies.

The only thing missing was the homemade cranberry sauce.

"We may *just* have enough. If not, we'll make do, won't we?" replied Grace, her eyes twinkling.

Belle chuckled and fetched the cranberry sauce from the stove.

Grace had been baking all morning too. There was a delicious-smelling apple pie cooling on the kitchen table, a fruit-cake that was being kept safe from Mittens in the pantry, and a chocolate cake with white frosting and red Christmas trees iced on top. She would take the fruit-cake and the chocolate cake to the local soup kitchen later, to donate to the local charity Christmas dinner for the town.

"I think we'll be eating leftovers for days," said Belle, rubbing her growling stomach.

"Exactly. That's half the fun of Christmas dinner." Grace laughed. "The leftovers."

Just then, Belle's cell phone buzzed.

"It's Harvey," Belle read the message with a smile. "He's parking outside."

"Wonderful!" said Grace. "Let's hope that he brought his appetite with him."

Belle chuckled and went to the front door to greet their visitor, Mittens at her heels.

Her boss stood there, shivering in the cold. A bright red scarf was wrapped around his neck and he had a knitted cap pulled over his ears. His eyes brightened when he saw Belle, and she opened the door to him with a smile.

"Hello!" said Belle as he stepped inside and handed her the bottle of wine that he was carrying.

"Merry Christmas!" said Harvey, giving her a quick hug.

"You too! Come on in. The party has already started."

Belle took his coat and hung it up in the closet by the door. Then she led him into the warm kitchen.

"Merry Christmas, Grace!" called Harvey as he walked in, breathing in the cooking smells with a hungry smile.

"Merry Christmas, Harvey!" said Grace, pulling him into a big hug. "What a lucky escape you've had. Good heavens!" She gave him a playful poke in the stomach. "And you're cold."

"It's below zero out there. Thank you for inviting me. This looks like a delicious feast. Much better than I would have got in the county lockup." Harvey looked pensive all of a sudden. "I'm still sad about what happened to Victoria. And on my farm too! I thought she was the one for me. I had no idea that she was married, until after I had loaned her all that money."

"My dear, you were only trying to help her, like you help so many people," said Grace, patting him on the arm.

"When I found out that she had a husband, I was so shocked that I immediately broke up with her. Now, I'll never know if she was really going to leave him or not." He took a deep breath. "It helps to know that justice has won and her killer is behind bars."

"Well now that Sheriff Barnes has closed the case, what are you going to do about your Christmas Tree Farm?" asked Grace, briskly changing the subject as she bustled about, getting plates and silverware for them all. "Belle mentioned the other day that you may have to sell your business."

The man's face brightened. "Not anymore. I'm going to expand it! Since Mr. Dunn is now in jail for what he did, he couldn't stop the sale of his house from going through. That meant the executor of Victoria Dunn's estate has claimed the money from the sale of his house to repay all of her debts. I have got all of my money back and my business is safe." Harvey looked better than Belle had seen him in a long time.

"What a relief!" exclaimed Belle, clapping her hands.

"Yes, it sure is. I'm going to use the money to pay off most of my mortgage and even buy some more acreage to expand my tree farm. It's going to be a lot of hard work, but it will be worth it."

A flush of happiness for Harvey flowed through Belle. It was good to see him excited about his plans for the future. It was something for him to focus on after all that he had gone through with Victoria.

"Thanks to your hot chocolate booth, Belle, my tree farm has a better reputation than before." He beamed. "I'm going to get a web design agency in town to help with my website. I have some photos of you working at the hot chocolate booth and we're going to feature them on the website. Next Christmas will be even more successful than this year!"

"That's wonderful. You deserve it after all the hard work you've put in," said Belle, pleased that she could help him out. "And I'm glad that my hot chocolate helped promote your trees."

Suddenly, the doorbell rang again. Belle and Grace exchanged a look.

"Who could that be?" said Belle, frowning.

Mittens raced to the door.

"I'll better protect whoever it is from the cat," said Belle, with an amused smile, heading out of the kitchen.

She was surprised to see Sheriff Barnes standing on her doorstep. He had a big covered dish in his hands and he held it up with a smile as soon as she opened the door.

"Sheriff Barnes, Merry Christmas! What are you doing here?" said Belle, a little shocked. "Don't tell me you have come to arrest someone else?"

"Merry Christmas to you too, Belle," he said. He glanced inside at the warming fire in the hearth and the deep green Christmas tree covered in red and gold tinsel. "I brought this gingerbread cobbler from the diner. I wanted to check on you after your experience in Hollydale."

"You didn't have to do that. I'm doing well. Thank you for worrying about me. This smells delicious!" She took the dish from him and lifted the towel that covered it. She inhaled deeply, the spicy scent making her mouth water.

"It's for both you and your grandmother," said the sheriff. "I hope you enjoy it."

"Thank you, Sheriff," said Belle, touched by his gesture.

Grace bustled in from the kitchen. "And you'll stay for lunch, Sheriff," she said in a way that brooked no argument.

"Oh, now..." said Sheriff Barnes with a smile, sneaking a peek toward the kitchen. He looked from Grace to Belle and back again. "Well, if you insist. My wife has planned a dinner later, but there's no reason why I can't enjoy a Christmas lunch too!"

Belle noticed a twinkle in his eye, as he took off his hat and stepped inside.

"I'll take your coat." Belle chuckled as she hung it up by the front door. Clearly, Cherryville's finest had wanted to see what Grace Beaumont had prepared for Christmas lunch. "Come on into the kitchen."

Belle hung the sheriff's coat and locked the front door against the snow. She returned to the kitchen in time to hear Grace ordering the two men to sit and make themselves comfortable.

"No hard feelings, hey, Harvey?" the sheriff said.

Harvey gave him a look. "You arrested me."

The sheriff shrugged. "Well, to my credit, I also helped get you released."

Harvey considered this for a moment and then smiled. True to his generous nature, he agreed. "No hard feelings, Sheriff Barnes."

"Come on, Mittens," said Belle with a smile at the cat, who was sitting by her side, begging shamelessly to get into the action somehow. "I'm sure there are some scraps for you."

They all passed around bowls and platters of food, while Harvey helped Grace carve the turkey. When all was served, they paused as Grace said a prayer of thanks for the food and for the company. Then they started eating.

"This is really the best Christmas lunch I've ever had," said Belle, with her mouth full of mashed potatoes.

"You said that last year, dear," said Grace.

"You're right; this is fabulous, Belle," said Harvey with a satisfied smile, as he reached for another slice of turkey. "Your grandmother is a fine cook."

"Yes, she is," said Belle with a contented sigh, as she poured more gravy over her plate.

The sheriff ate like a man starved. He was obviously enjoying himself. And he would eat a second Christmas meal in a few hours too.

"I have to say, I didn't think I would have such a merry Christmas this year. I thought I would be on duty through the holidays because of the Dunn case," he said, with a nod at Harvey. "But all's well that ends well."

"Thanks to Belle and her investigating skills," said Harvey, lifting his chin in her direction.

"Yes, thanks to Belle." The sheriff assumed a serious expression. "She was instrumental in getting to the bottom of Victoria Dunn's murder. We got the entire conversation that she had with Mr. Dunn on tape."

Belle blushed. She didn't think of herself as an investigator. She just wanted to help Harvey and the town. It felt good to know that she had done that.

"To family," said Grace with a smile, lifting her glass of iced tea.

"And to friends," added Sheriff Barnes, with a nod at Harvey.

"And to Mittens!" said Belle, raising her glass too.

Mittens stopped chewing his scraps and meowed in agreement.

Everyone laughed. Belle looked around the table at the merry faces of the people that she cared about. She had so much to be thankful for.

It had turned out to be a very merry Christmas after all!

Chapter 21

Homicide and a Happy New Year. Coming soon!

"Goodness, I think I've eaten too much again," said Grace Beaumont, yawning as she put her feet up on a padded footrest. "I can't believe that I finished the last of the Christmas cookies." She smoothed her hand over her stomach." I'm really going to have to start working out more."

Flames from a burning log popped and crackled merrily in the fireplace. Mittens, who was curled up on the mat in front of the fire, stretched and yawned too.

Belle glanced over at her petite grandmother and chuckled. "For goodness' sake, Gram. You're as thin as ever. Plus, you do so much, that it is hard for anyone to keep up with you!"

Grace huffed. "You're just saying that because you know I'll make *you* my personal trainer."

Belle laughed again. "I think that you're perfect just the way you are."

Grace reached over to pat her granddaughter's hand. "I think that you're perfect just the way you are, too." She yawned again and close your eyes for a moment.

"Thanks, Gram," Belle replied, her forehead creasing with concern before she turned her gaze back to the flames dancing in the fireplace.

She had noticed that, despite all of her baking activities, Gram was increasingly tired these days. It was to be expected. Over the past year, her slow-growing cancer had required regular treatments at the local clinic. Thankfully, things were in remission. For now. She could go for longer periods without a visit to her doctor. However, Belle still lived in a constant state of alert, in case the dreaded condition returned.

And then there were the medical bills.

To say that being sick was not cheap, would be an understatement. The costs of Gram's hospital visits had been more than Belle had expected. Her brain was constantly working on how to make sure that they had enough money to pay the debt every month. It felt like trying to solve an elusive clue for a crossword puzzle, but never quite getting the answer.

"I'm glad everyone had a good time on Christmas Day," said Grace from her recliner as she sipped her snowberry tea. "It's lovely having visitors, but it's even better when you can sit by your own fire and relax. Now that it's just the two of us, we can celebrate however we want." She tucked the little crocheted blanket around her legs with a happy sigh.

Mittens meowed in agreement and took the opportunity of jumping up onto Grace's lap. He focusing on making himself comfortable, his little feet kneading the blanket.

Belle picked up her tea and sipped it. She snuggled deeper under her knitted blanket and watched the pine cones in the fire crackle and pop. She had collected them from the local park back in autumn and had added them to their woodpile. Now the sweet smell of pine filled the house.

It was Boxing Day, the day after Christmas, and Belle was enjoying having some time off. After working non-stop at the hot chocolate booth for the last six weeks, it was nice to relax and take a break.

The Christmas tree was still in the corner of the living room, its green boughs laden with wooden ornaments, tinsel, and lights. Soon, they would need to take down the decorations and pack them away in the garage. But not yet.

Belle's eyes fell upon the star at the top of the tree, its wooden surface painted with gold paint, now a little scratched and worn. She had made it herself with the help of her Gram several years ago.

It was a tradition in Belle's family to put up a Christmas tree early every year and to spend time together making decorations to add to their collection. Even though her parents had passed away when Belle was quite young, her grandmother had carried on the tradition. This year they had made two little dangly icicles and two glittering snowflakes, from sparkly beads and sequins. The new decorations caught the light from the fire and reflected it onto the wall in dancing patterns.

Unfortunately, Mittens also loved the glittery new decorations, possibly a little too much. He liked trying to climb the Christmas tree too. Belle and Grace usually spent a few minutes of every morning picking the fallen decorations up and hanging them back on the tree.

Outside, the snow was gently falling, blanketing the town in a soft white eiderdown of cold fluff. Through the window, Belle could see their twinkly lights strung out on the porch banister, winking on and off.

Grace had picked up her knitting and her needles clicked and clacked together as she worked on a new project, a scarf for Belle. Belle watched her grandmother working the needles, admiring her nimble fingers.

"So, what are you going to do now, Belle?" Grace stroked Mittens, who had was purring loudly. "Your year was very busy with different jobs, but it's over now. What are you going to do next?"

It was true. Belle's work at the hot chocolate booth at Harvey's Christmas Tree Farm was finished. Instead of selling Christmas trees, Harvey was now busily planting new ones for the coming years. He had offered Belle short-term work sorting out his messy office, but that work may only be available in a few weeks' time. Plus, as soon as his office was tidy, there would be no more need for Belle's services and then she would be back to square one, looking for employment.

Belle gazed into the fire. "I really don't know," she admitted.

She had been thinking about it for some time now, but every time she tried to come up with an idea, nothing seemed right. "I'm going to look for a job in a couple of days," she added. She set her cup of tea on the table beside the couch. She had tried not to think about it too much. But if Belle was honest, the thought of what she would do next had been worrying her a little. Not that she wanted her grandmother to know that. The last thing she wanted her Gram to do was worry about money. "There will be lots of places hiring when the new year starts. We'll just have to watch our pennies until then."

"You're right. At least we have my pension," said Grace, finishing her row of stitches, turning her knitting and starting another row. "I was thinking that I could ask the women at the Guild whether they know of anyone needing to hire staff."

"The Cherryville Women's Guild?" Belle wrinkled her nose. "I think that it would be better not to get them involved."

The Women's Guild was an organization of women who met once a week to knit, crochet, and gossip like old hens. Grace went there every week for the companionship and the conversation. Conversation that usually involved small-town news and gossip.

For instance, the Women's Guild had once gotten wind that the new girl in town, an artist named Bonnie, was looking for a boyfriend. They had immediately tried to match her up with every one of their sons and nephews. The poor woman had been sent on so many blind dates that she had desperately signed up for online dating just to get away from their well-intentioned introductions. In no time, Bonnie had found a boyfriend for herself. One who lived in another town. She had headed out of town as fast as possible, her car packed to the roof with all her possessions.

"But they might know of someone who is hiring," persisted Grace. "It can't hurt to ask."

"It sure could," said Belle. "You know Wilma and her organizational abilities. She'll call a town meeting to discuss my job opportunities. Before we know it, everyone in Cherryville will know about our business." Wilma was the President of the Women's Guild and she liked to organize the lives of everyone in town, usually to their detriment. Unfortunately, Wilma's enthusiasm for helping people, whether they wanted the help or not, usually ended up in a complete mess. "I don't want people knowing what's going on with us or offering me weird jobs."

Grace smiled. She had only been half serious about involving the Women's Guild in finding Belle a new job. "Okay. I won't ask Wilma to find you a job. But I really wish that I could help bring in money for my medical bills. I wish that I could go back to teaching, but I just don't have the energy anymore."

Grace had previously worked as a teacher at the local high school, and the children had adored her. But she had retired a few years ago when her health started to decline.

"There are plenty of other things that you could do," said Belle, trying to think of ways to cheer her up. "You're always so good at crafts. Why don't you sell them online?"

"Oh, I don't know," said Grace, stroking Mittens' soft fur as he lay purring in the crook of her arm. "I really enjoy doing my crafts in my own time, rather than for a deadline. I don't think my arthritic fingers could keep up with that much knitting."

She picked up her a flyer and handed it to Belle. "But I could always apply for this job at the winery," she joked. "Or you could. You're good at making friends."

"The winery?" asked Belle, frowning at the flyer in the dim light from the fire. "Would that be the Buchen Winery? That fancy place just out of town?" She turned over the page.

The flyer was indeed for the Buchen Winery. They were hosting a New Year's celebration, and they were looking for staff for the party and then to work for the whole of January, serving wine to tourists. She had heard about the Buchen Winery, but to be honest, it was too fancy a place for many of the blue-collar people of Cherryville to visit. Plus, Mr Buchen hired most of their staff from out of state. She didn't know anyone who had worked there. The Buchen Winery was a bit of an enigma. "Well, as long as there are no dead bodies for me to find in unexpected places. That sounds perfect!" joked Belle.

After discovering the dead body of a woman in a dumpster at her last job, and helping the sheriff to catch the killer, Belle was looking for a job that was boring and normal. "There have been no murders at the Buchen Winery, have there?"

"No. Not that I know of. But it said something in here about understanding wines," said her grandmother, taking the paper back and squinting at the small print. "What does that mean? How much is there to understand? You open the bottle and you drink it."

Belle shrugged. "I guess there are different wines to learn about. It says that they're willing to train the right people."

"Well, if you're sure," said her Gram, frowning. "It would be a change from working outside in the cold. Better than running a hot chocolate booth in the snow."

Belle smiled. "It would." The warmth from the fireplace was soothing, and she could feel her eyelids getting heavy. She yawned and stretched.

"You could phone them tomorrow morning," said Grace, handing back the paper as the hall clock chimed ten times. She nodded at Belle's nearly empty mug of tea. "I think it's time for bed."

Belle got up from the couch, folded the knitted blanket, and gave Mittens a pat. "Okay, I'm going to sleep. I'll see you in the morning."

"Okay, goodnight," said her Gram, smiling as she got to her feet to give Belle a hug. "Sleep well, my dear."

As Belle got ready for bed, she pondered what she would need in order to serve wines. A uniform, for sure. No doubt she would be required to wear all black, like the restaurants that she had worked in before. She thought of the bills that were due in January and wondered how much the Buchen Winery paid their short-term staff. The prospect of working at a winery intrigued her too. It would be a fun change and she would get to learn more about wines. Even better, it would be a normal job that didn't involve standing in the snow or solving murders.

Belle read the job advert again and circled the number for the winery with a pen. She would call them first thing tomorrow morning. The advert said a short phone interview was all that was needed.

As she switched off her bedside lamp, Mittens jumped onto the end of her bed.

"How much do you know about wines?" she asked him in the darkness.

Mittens purred in response.

"Me either," she said. "But then again, how hard could it be?"

About the Author

Ellie McDougan is a pen name for an author who grew up in Africa, then studied and traveled a lot before settling down. This has come in handy for her writing, as she likes to include some elements of different countries in her mysteries. She writes about women who work in many different jobs yet seem to find themselves solving crimes at them all. If you love cozy mysteries with a touch of humor, you'll love her books!

Ellie now lives in Australia with three cats, all of which she adores. When she's not writing or spending time with her felines, she enjoys reading stories about solving crimes (of course), studying some more, starting slightly skewed sewing projects but never finishing them, and watching DIY videos on Youtube that no one should try at home. Trust her, she's tried them.

Read more at https://elliemcdougan.com/.

www.ingramcontent.com/pod-product-compliance
Lightning Source LLC
Chambersburg PA
CBHW071320130626
46556CB00004B/1680